Stagecoach to Damnation

What should have been a normal uneventful stagecoach run from Stoneville to the town of Damnation soon became a nightmare. It began with a bad omen when the mad Indian started following the stage. Then the bank robber Sterne turned up, but even worse was yet to come with the appearance of the psychopath Wakely.

And so it was that the rest of the passengers on the stage were merely innocent people dragged into a truly frightening series of events.

Now it was all up to Grayling, the shotgun rider, to put his life on the line. But could just one brave man restore law and order? Or would it all end in a bloody showdown?

By the same author

Showdown in Hawkesville
Lowry's Revenge
Guns Over Adamsville
Texan Bounty Hunter
Mountain Guns
Gunsmoke Over Eden
Ambush Valley

Stagecoach to Damnation

RON WATKINS

A Black Horse Western

ROBERT HALE · LONDON

© Ron Watkins 2001
First published in Great Britain 2001

ISBN 0 7090 6859 X

Robert Hale Limited
Clerkenwell House
Clerkenwell Green
London EC1R 0HT

The right of Ron Watkins to be identified as
author of this work has been asserted by him
in accordance with the Copyright, Designs and
Patents Act 1988.

Typeset by
Derek Doyle & Associates, Liverpool
Printed and bound in Great Britain by
Antony Rowe Ltd, Wiltshire

For granddaughter number six – Lucy Victoria

1

'Anyone for the stage?'

The stranger, whose name was Grayling, stood in the doorway of the Red Garter saloon. Normally the dozen or so early regulars in the saloon would have ignored him and carried on either with their game of cards or with their conversations, but there was something about the tone of his clipped request that made some of them glance at him.

They saw a tall lean man dressed in black. They noticed that his holster was tied down and that he also carried a sheath knife. He had a weather-beaten hard face with pale-blue eyes. It was the face of a man who didn't often smile.

'I'm looking for a man named Callaway,' said Grayling. 'Is he here?'

The barman, a burly man named Styles answered. 'No, he isn't here.'

Stagecoach to Damnation

'You know him?' demanded Grayling.

'Sure. Everybody in town knows him. He's the town drunk.'

'Why is he catching the stage?' asked one of the regulars. 'Normally he doesn't travel far from one of the saloons.'

'Maybe he wants to get away from temptation,' suggested his companion.

'By going to Damnation?' demanded the other, scornfully. 'Anybody living there would need twice as much to drink to survive in that hellhole.'

'I take it nobody's seen him,' said Grayling, drily.

'Why don't you try the other five saloons in town?' asked the barman. 'You'll surely find him in one of them.'

'I already have,' said Grayling curtly, as he turned on his heel. 'He isn't in any of them.'

'Well?' demanded the stage driver when Grayling returned to the waiting stage.

'No sign of him.'

'All right, we can't wait any longer,' said the driver, whose name was Lawson. 'It'll just mean we'll have one less passenger.'

Grayling jumped up on the buckboard. He checked that his two rifles – the Winchester and the shotgun – were safely tucked underneath. 'I'm ready,' he said.

Stagecoach to Damnation

At that moment there was a shrill whistle from someone a short distance behind. 'Hold it,' said a man who was hurrying towards the stagecoach. He was a middle-aged man who was carrying his hat in his hand as he ran. He reached the stage, panting loudly. 'I hear you're a passenger short,' he gasped.

'It's nothing to do with us,' said Lawson. 'We don't do the bookings. You'll have to call in at the office.'

'I already have,' said the other, triumphantly holding up a ticket.

Lawson glanced at the ticket. He saw that it was made out in the name of Smythe. 'Callaway must have cancelled,' he informed Grayling. 'He must have had second thoughts about going to Damnation.' He addressed the new arrival. 'Have you got any luggage?'

'No,' was the reply.

'Jump on then,' said the driver, curtly. When Smythe had joined the other five passengers, he cracked his whip. 'All set?' he asked the man by his side.

'Sure,' replied Grayling.

Lawson slowly released the brake and the stage started on its journey. It was eighteen miles to Herford and a further forty to Damnation. The driver had been doing the trip for the past six months or so without any serious mishaps. True there had been the occasional sightings of wandering gangs of Indians, but usually a few warning shots in their direction had been sufficient to deter them from wandering near the stage. In fact the sightings of the Indians had come to be regarded by many of the passengers as one of the thrills which helped to make up for the discomfort and boredom of the stage ride. Some passengers had been heard to express disappointment that they had made the whole trip without seeing a single Indian.

The coach moved slowly down Main Street with its complement of half a dozen passengers. They would spend five days in the coach, travelling six hours a day in a cramped, uncomfortable seat in which, as the temperature inside the coach rose with the passing miles would become hotter and even more cramped and uncomfortable. As the coach passed the sheriff's office the deputy sheriff watched it from the doorway. The sheriff came out to join him.

'I wonder what happened to Callaway?' asked the sheriff. 'He booked his ticket a week ago. He was full of his journey to Damnation at that time.'

'More likely he was full of whiskey too,' stated the deputy.

'I expect you're right,' stated the sheriff. 'He probably changed his mind. Nobody in their right senses would be eager to go to Damnation.'

However a few hours later the real reason for Callaway's non-appearance on the stage emerged. A young woman who had visited the local cemetery in order to lay some flowers on her late husband's grave was shocked to find the body of a man lying on the path. The man was lying face downward and had obviously been shot in the back of the head. She ran to the sheriff's office; when the sheriff arrived on the scene he turned the body over.

'It's Callaway,' he announced. He noticed a piece of paper sticking out of the corpse's pocket. Carefully pulling it out he stared at it with more than a little surprise. It was the ticket which Callaway should have presented to travel on the coach that morning.

2

A small crowd had gathered on an open space on the outskirts of the town. They were watching a man who called himself Ed Smith trying to sell them home made medicines. Ed was a short, stocky man in his late forties with brown eyes set in a square face. He was clean-shaven with short, cropped hair and he fancied himself as a ladies' man.

'See this,' he addressed the onlookers, holding a medicine bottle up high, 'this will get rid of colds, sneezes, rheumatics, headaches, boils, and all kinds of rashes.'

'Will it get rid of my wife?' asked a wag from the front.

'You'll need two bottles for that,' said Ed, holding one in each hand.

The small crowd roared with laughter. Ed felt the inward glow which comes to the outdoor trader when he knows he's got his audience in

Stagecoach to Damnation

the palm of his hand.

'You said it will cure boils,' said a man who was wearing a dark suit.

'That's right.' Ed turned slightly in order to face him.

'My brother has got boils. What does he do to cure them?'

It was a reccurring question which Ed had been asked many times on his travels. He assumed that the high percentage of people with boils was due to a lack of something or other in the people's diets, but he wisely said nothing about it.

'Take two spoonfuls of Doctor Smith's balsam every morning and night until he's taken the whole bottle. When he's taken it all he'll find that the boils have disappeared.'

'How much is it?' demanded the man.

'Fifty cents, that's all I'm asking.'

Several of the crowd were obviously considering buying the balsam. A skinny teenage girl spoke up from the back of the crowd. 'My mother sent me to buy a bottle. She said it cured her when she had influenza.'

'Here's someone who's got faith in my balsam,' cried Ed, as he exchanged a bottle for fifty cents.

It was obviously that moment which swayed those in the audience who had been undecided whether to buy it or not. Several now came forward with their money.

Stagecoach to Damnation

The instructions are on the label,' said Ed, as he handed over the bottles.

In a short while the crowd had dispersed. Ed mopped his brow. He turned and stepped up into the covered wagon. The teenager who had bought the bottle of balsam reappeared and glanced around cautiously. Satisfied that there was no one in sight she crossed over to the wagon. She pulled up the flap and stepped inside. Ed was sitting on a stool drinking whiskey.

'Have you got to drink that stuff, Pa?' she said, disapprovingly.

She was in her late teens and if she had been wearing a dress that fitted instead of the shapeless reject she was wearing would have been quite attractive. Her hair too required some attention, the minimum of which would have been a ribbon to hold the unruly mop in place.

'A man's got to have something to help him relax,' said Ed, wiping his mouth with the back of his hand. 'Anyhow, Harriet, this stuff could be the thing that saves our bacon,' he said, holding up the glass and examining it critically.

'Not if you keep drinking it,' she said sharply as she fished a biscuit-tin out from a cupboard and began nibbling at one.

'You don't want to keep going around from town to town for ever and a day, do you?' he asked. 'You want to settle down somewhere and lead a normal life, don't you?'

'A fat chance of that,' she said, choosing another biscuit.

'You'd like to live in a house instead of in this wagon, wear a nice dress and have some friends the way other teenagers do, wouldn't you?'

'We did have a house once,' she said, curtly. 'And I wore nice dresses, and had friends like other girls.'

'Yes, well I admit I went to pieces after your mother died,' he said, with more than a hint of sadness in his voice. 'Then I had a bit of bad luck with the cards—'

'And so we've been on the road for the last two years,' she interrupted.

'I said I'd make it up to you, didn't I? With this stuff we'll be making far more than the paltry fifty cents we make with the balsam. I'm ready to start selling this,' he held up the glass. 'Three dollars a bottle. What do you think of that?'

'And how many do you think you'll sell?'

'We'll see. We'll start tomorrow.'

'So we'd better think of moving.'

'No we'll stay here. Herford seems a nice peaceful town. It's just the place for us to settle down. When we've made enough money, we'll rent a house. Everything will be back to what it was, you'll see,' he said, emptying his whiskey glass.

3

The six passengers in the stage, having in the first place glanced curiously at their companions, were now looking studiously out at the scenery. Two of the passengers were related, in fact they were husband and wife, Mr and Mrs Beeson, although the husband preferred the more formal title – the Reverend. He wore a dog-collar and the pair were intending to set up a church in Damnation. When they had heard the name of the town they had both gone down on their knees and prayed to the Lord. To their delight the Lord had answered their prayers and had told them to travel to Damnation and save souls for him. After all, with a name like Damnation there must be hundreds of souls in the town just waiting to be saved. It was a short time after they arrived at the town that they discovered the name had nothing to do with the number of souls on their

Stagecoach to Damnation

way to purgatory, but with the inclement climate to which the town was regularly subjected.

In addition to Mrs Beeson there was one other lady on the stage. She was about half Mrs Beeson's age and about twice as pretty. The lady's name was Doris Thompson. Mrs Beeson had instantly observed that she was wearing no wedding- or engagement-ring. And that furthermore, she was wearing a dress which was distinctly low cut. Mrs Beeson pursed her lips and decided that if Miss Thompson was travelling all the way to Damnation she would be especially marked out as somebody who would receive the 'word of the Lord' – together with advice not to wear a dress which was cut so low and which could inflame men's passions.

Seated on the other side of the stage were three men. Their ages varied from the youngest – a young man barely out of his teens named Sam Melrose, to the middle-aged man who had been a late arrival on the stage whose name was Clay Sterne, to a white-haired man whose name was Leonard Bridges. He looked the most prosperous of the three, with his gold watch conspicuously tucked in his waistcoat, and was in fact a banker. The only one wearing a revolver was Clay Sterne.

The four horses slowly ate up the miles. Up on the buckboard no words passed between Cam Grayling and Lawson. The only sound apart from the clatter of the horses' hoofs on the trail and the rumble of the coach's wheels was the noisy sound of Lawson chewing. It was beginning to get on Cam's nerves. Finally he said, 'Are you going to make a noise chewing all the way to Herford?'

'Always have done. Don't intend to stop now,' said Lawson, spitting accurately between the horses.

Cam realized he would have to put up with it for the rest of the journey. The driver was the person in charge of the stage; he was merely the shotgun rider. He sighed and turned his attention to the scenery. He decided it was as uninviting as Lawson's face. They were driving through a wide valley of scrub grass with hills rising on either side. There were no animals in sight. The hills, although they appeared greener than the sandy-coloured valley, obviously didn't support grazing animals. He hoped the rest of the journey wouldn't be as boring as the present scenery.

He would have been surprised if he had known that back in Stoneville the sheriff and his deputy were discussing the stage, or rather one particular person on it.

'What do we know about him?' asked the sheriff.

'Nothing,' replied his deputy. 'Except that he joined the stage here in Stoneville.'

Stagecoach to Damnation

'I've sent a telegraph to the Wells Fargo office. I've asked for any information they have on Cam Grayling. We should have a reply shortly. I still don't see why anyone should kill Callaway,' he added, thoughtfully. 'What would they gain out of it?'

'Perhaps it's one of those people who are against drunks,' suggested the deputy. 'What do they call them – teetotallers.'

'That's not funny,' snapped the sheriff.

His deputy was used to the sheriff's sudden swings of mood. 'Maybe there's another possibility about Callaway,' he said to divert the sheriff's anger.

'What's that?' growled the other.

'That one of the other passengers killed him. The one who took his place on the stage.'

'You mean that could have been the reason for Callaway getting killed,' said the sheriff, thoughtfully, his sudden burst of anger having subsided as quickly as it started.

'It's a possibility.'

4

The stage reached the first staging-post without mishap and with very little conversation between those inside the stage and also the two on the buckboard. The staging-post was run by an old couple named Cooper and after the passengers had alighted Mrs Cooper informed them that washing facilities had been provided in the separate rooms at the back of the single storey building. She had filled the large porcelain baths with warm water. She was a garrulous old lady and informed them how she could always see the dust from the stage when it was a couple of miles away. This gave her time to fill the baths with warm water.

Later the passengers filed into the dining-room. Mrs Cooper had prepared a stew which smelled delicious. However, to the annoyance of some of the passengers, particularly the youngster Sam Melrose, they were not allowed to tuck

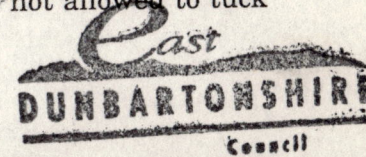

in until the reverend had concluded a lengthy grace.

After the meal most of the passengers headed for their bunks, since Lawson had informed them that they were due to make an early start in the morning. Cam went out on the porch to have a smoke. To his surprise he was able to smell a whiff of perfume and realized that Miss Thompson was standing at the other end of the porch.

'Do you mind if I join you?' she asked. 'I always like the smell of a cigar.'

Cam, who had been hoping for a quiet smoke, realized he couldn't refuse. 'No,' he replied, 'I don't mind.'

'By the way,' she said, as she moved closer to him, 'my name is Doris.'

'I know,' said Cam, shortly, 'I saw it on your ticket.'

'And your name is Cam Grayling. Somebody told me,' she said, ignoring his curtness.

Cam smoked his cigar in silence.

'Have you done this run before?' she asked, breaking the silence.

'No,' replied Cam.

'I see. So you're not a regular shotgun rider?'

'I didn't say that.'

'You don't say a lot, do you?' she retorted, with some irritation.

Stagecoach to Damnation

'No,' answered Cam.

'Well, since you're obviously not going to tell me your life story, maybe you'd like to hear mine. I'm a dressmaker, and I also make hats. I'm telling you this because it might have some bearing on a yell you might hear on the next run tomorrow morning.'

'What do you mean?' asked Cam, with sudden interest.

'Oh, it won't be coming from me. It'll be coming from that skunk who's sitting next to me.'

'The preacher?' asked Cam.

'Yes, he's also a dirty old man. He keeps rubbing up against my leg.'

'Are you sure you're not imagining it? After all, it's a bumpy ride in the stage.'

'Of course I'm not imagining it,' she snapped. 'I've been around. I know when a man is rubbing against me.'

'Maybe it's not surprising.'

'What's that supposed to mean?' she bristled.

'Nothing, except that you're an attractive young lady,' he said, glancing at her. 'And I would guess that lots of men have made advances to you in your time.'

'This isn't an advance. Unless he beats a retreat he'll have a hatpin stuck into his anatomy tomorrow.' She paused. 'That's where you come in,' she said, glancing up at him.

Stagecoach to Damnation

'It's nothing to do with me. I'm not even in charge of the stage.'

'That's right. Like most men you don't want to know when a woman's in danger,' she said, bitterly.

'I'd hardly call it being in danger when you're sitting in a stage with five other people. Even though one of them might be rubbing up against you,' he reminded her.

'I'm telling you he is,' she said emphatically.

He sighed. 'All right, what do you want me to do?'

'Before the coach starts tomorrow I want you to get one of my boxes down from the roof. It's the one with some hats in it. It's also got a few hatpins. I want to get one of them out. The reverend will have a shock coming to him if he tries his tricks tomorrow.'

Cam finished his cigar and stubbed it out on the porch rail before throwing it away. 'All right, I'll see what I can do,' he said, as he turned away. 'I'm going to turn in. Oh, and Miss Thomson—'

'Call me Doris,' she interrupted.

'All right – Doris – I'd turn in too if I were you. Snakes often come out at night. Rattlers, sidewinders—'

'I aim to deal with a snake called the Reverend tomorrow,' she retorted.

5

The stage was on its way early. Before breakfast Cam had met Doris outside and had fetched the hatbox down from the top of the stage. He had watched while she had opened it and selected a suitable hatpin. 'This should put him off,' she informed Cam, as she closed the box.

The horses needed no second hint to the *crack* of the whip before beginning to pull away from the staging-post. The pale sun promised that it would soon change into a deeper yellow when it began its slow climb. Cam tried to make his long legs as comfortable as he could on the journey ahead to Herford.

They were soon following the long monotonous valley they had left the previous day. Lawson opened his first packet of chewing-tobacco. This time he did not offer any to his companion on the buckboard. Cam, although he did not expect trouble from any sources outside the stage still kept his eyes peeled on the hills on either side of the wide valley.

They had travelled about a couple of miles and the sun was beginning to make its presence felt when the two on the buckboard heard an unholy yell from inside the stage. Lawson was instantly about to apply the brake when Cam reached out a restraining hand. 'I don't think it's worth pulling up for,' he informed him.

'Sounds as though someone's being murdered,' said Lawson.

'It's just a bit of fun and games. Although come to think of maybe someone will get murdered when his wife gets him home.'

'The preacher?' queried Lawson.

'Exactly. He's been rubbing up against Miss Thompson. Although I don't think he'll do it again.'

In the coach there was hullabaloo. Mrs Beeson was screaming at Doris for stabbing her husband with a hatpin. Doris, who was no less vociferous, was shouting that she wouldn't have stabbed him if he hadn't kept rubbing up against her. The reverend, who was purple with a combination of embarrassment and pain was trying ineffectively to deny the charge. The three men on the other side of the coach were looking on with undisguised interest. The row was finally settled by Leonard Bridges, the banker, suggest-

Stagecoach to Damnation

ing that Doris could change seats with one of the men on his side. She agreed. The young man, Sam Melrose, changed seats with her and so eventually she found herself seated next to Mr Bridges.

'You're safe with me,' he said with a wink. 'My interest in the opposite sex was over years ago.'

Mrs Beeson's glare could have killed a rabbit at twenty paces.

After that confrontation the journey settled down to its usual uneventful slow progress. Cam was still smiling at the episode a few minutes later and Lawson showed it had affected his own methodical mastication by biting off another chew.

It was an hour or so later when they spotted the Indian. He was on a black horse and had appeared over the top of the hill to the right of the stage.

'Indian,' said Cam, indicating to Lawson the direction of the unexpected new arrival.

Lawson glanced in the direction Cam had indicated. He grunted. Cam noticed that although the driver had appeared unconcerned about the Indian, he nevertheless kept glancing in his direction at regular intervals.

It took those in the stage longer to register the presence of the Indian. When they did there was an excited hubbub. It culminated in the young man, Sam Melrose, putting his head out through the window.

'Hey, there's an Indian following us,' he informed the two on the buckboard.

'We know,' replied Lawson. His other answer was to pull a sheath from the side of his seat. At first Cam thought that it held some sort of weapon, but when Lawson handed it to him, he saw that there was a telescope inside. Cam focused it on the Indian. To his surprise the face that sprang into view was wearing full war paint.

'Either he likes dressing up or he's going to a war dance,' he informed Lawson. He handed it to the driver who held the reins between his knees while he studied the Indian through the telescope.

'It's the first time I've seen one wearing full war paint on this run,' said Lawson. 'Better not tell those inside,' he added.

In fact the passengers had their own telescope. Leonard Bridges was the owner. 'He's wearing war paint,' he informed the others.

'What does that mean?' asked the reverend's wife, nervously.

'We'll be all right dear,' said her husband, who was delighted at the change of focus of attention from Doris to the Indian on the hilltop. They all watched as the Indian made no effort to go ahead of them, but was content to move along with them at their slow pace.

After a while the novelty of their unexpected watcher began to be replaced by concern among those in the stage. 'Can't you do something about him?' Mrs Beeson called out to the two on the buckboard.

'It's all right dear,' said her husband, this time venturing as far as to pat her hand.

'It's not all right,' she said, snatching her hand away. 'There's a savage over there, who's keeping an eye on us.'

'We're all God's creatures, dear,' her husband reminded her.

'For all we know he's just a look-out,' she continued, as if he hadn't spoken. 'There may be dozens of others on the other side of the hill.'

For the first time the expressions on the others' faces changed from concern to apprehension. 'You could be right,' said Clay. He drew his gun as if to reassure the others by its very presence.

The other five stared at the Colt as though it was a strange animal that had suddenly appeared in their midst.

'Can't you do something?' Mrs Beeson snapped the question at her husband.

The reverend cleared his throat. 'Driver,' he called out in his best pulpit voice. 'Can't you get rid of that Indian? Some of the people down here

Stagecoach to Damnation

are worried about the way he's trailing us.'

'I can't fire at him,' replied Cam. 'It could disturb the horses. Anyhow he's not doing any harm.'

'Not doing any harm,' screeched Mrs Beeson. 'We could all be scalped in our seats.'

'He's like the albatross in the poem *The Ancient Mariner*,' said Bridges. 'Only he was following a ship.'

'What happened in the end?' demanded Sam Melrose.

'The Ancient Mariner shot him,' said the other.

'You mean like this,' said Clay, taking aim out through the window.

'You're not going to kill him, are you?' protested Doris. 'After all, he's only following us.'

'I've got as much chance of hitting him as I'd have of shooting a bull's balls off at a couple of hundred yards,' said Clay. 'All I intend to do is to scare him off.'

He suited his action to the words. He fired the Colt. The sound inside the coach was deafening. The horses at first lost their stride, then they pricked up their ears and began to gallop as if a horde of Indians was firing at them.

The passengers inside the coach held on in consternation as the coach swayed and rattled along.

'That was a stupid thing to do,' said Bridges.

'I got rid of him though, didn't I?' Clay pointed out.

True enough there was now no sign of the Indian. However Clay's triumph at getting rid of the Indian was short-lived. The coach gave a sudden sickening lurch, balanced on two wheels for what seemed like an eternity then jerked back upright as the horses involuntarily slowed down. There came a grinding, rasping noise as one of the wheels parted company from its axle, the coach ending up at a crazy angle.

'That's torn it,' Lawson summed it up.

In Stoneville the sheriff and his deputy were discussing an official piece of paper which lay on the desk in front of them. It was a telegram which the deputy had collected from the telegraph office.

'So Clay Sterne is wanted for robbery and murder,' stated the sheriff, glancing at the telegram for the third time as though finally to dispel any lingering doubts about its veracity.

'That's what the county marshal says,' replied the other.

'He doesn't say what he expects us to do about it.'

'He's left it up to you. He'll know you'll make the right decision.' The deputy made the remark knowing that the sheriff was too stupid to appreciate the sarcasm in it.

'I wonder if Sterne operates on his own, or is he

a member of a gang?' said the sheriff thoughtfully.

'We won't know,' said his deputy. 'I've looked through all the Wanted notices, but I can't find out anything about him.'

'Of course the stage is outside our limits by now. Officially we can't do anything about it,' stated the sheriff.

'No, I suppose not.' His deputy pretended to agree, although inwardly he was bursting with eagerness to go after the robber. However he knew that the last thing to do would be to betray any emotion which might reveal this aim. Should the sheriff realize that he was set on going after Clay it would be a dollar to a cent that he would keep him in the office. In his opinion the sheriff was not only stupid but he was a spiteful, cantankerous old fool.

'On the other hand it would be a feather in our cap if we captured Clay,' said the sheriff, after due consideration.

The deputy's heart skipped a beat. This was what he had been hoping to hear. He managed to keep a straight face with an effort.

'It might even mean an increase in your pension when you retire,' suggested the deputy, sagaciously.

'Yeah, that's a possibility.' The sheriff considered it for a few moments. His deputy held his

Stagecoach to Damnation

breath. Finally he heard the words he had been hoping to hear. 'You'd better go after the stage. I won't telegraph Herford to let them know that they can expect a killer on the stage. If you get a move on you should catch the stage before it reaches the town. Bring him back alive so that he can stand trial. We might find out then if there are any other members in his gang.'

'Right, I'll be on my way,' said the deputy, buckling on his gunbelt.

'And don't take any chances, remember he's a killer,' were the sheriff's final parting words of advice.

In fact the deputy was rather surprised by those final remarks. His relationship with the sheriff had generally been one of concealed hostility, and he had assumed that the sheriff felt the same about him – maybe because the sheriff realized he was mentally his inferior. Certainly in the latter's outbursts of anger he had left him in no doubt that he would never qualify as the best deputy he had ever had. But maybe the sheriff had a hidden streak of the milk of human kindness which he hadn't suspected. When he came back he'd make it up by ordering those cigars he liked.

Actually the reason for the sheriff's remark was that he didn't want his deputy to go blundering in and make a dog's dinner of the whole affair. Although the telegram didn't say so, he guessed there would be a bounty on Clay's head. If his deputy succeeded in bringing him in alive it would be an easy matter to arrange to have Clay killed while trying to escape from jail. That way he, the sheriff, would claim the whole bounty. It was a good thing the deputy was too stupid to have grasped that point.

The horses were grazing near the broken stage. They had been the driver's first concern. After quickly ushering the passengers out he and Clay had slipped the horses out of the shafts and the driver had examined them critically before pronouncing them unharmed. His next action had been to examine the broken spindle.

'Do you think you can fix it?' asked Bridges.

'Yes, I think so,' replied the driver. 'Although it will take about half an hour.'

'As long as you can fix it, that's the main thing,' stated the other, with relief.

The rest were all standing around. 'Why don't you all have a bite to eat while I see to it,' suggested Lawson.

They brought out the biscuits which the old lady at the staging-post had supplied them with and seated themselves around the stage. The driver produced a long strip of rawhide. He began to cut it into a few smaller strips. Then he took his canteen and began to soak the rawhide.

'I'll tie these strips around the spindle,' he informed Bridges, who was watching him interestedly. 'Then when they dry they'll tighten. Hopefully it will fit well enough to get us to Herford. As my father used to say, there's nothing you can't fix with a knife and a length of rawhide.'

'I'll just go up that hill to see if that Indian is still around,' said Cam, after making sure that Lawson could manage without his help. He suited the action to his words by starting to climb the hill carrying his Winchester with him.

He didn't expect the Indian would still be around, nevertheless he slowed his stride to the careful movements of a stalker as he approached the top of the hill. Still taking no chances he dropped to the ground as he topped the hill.

As he had expected there was no sign of any human life, and very little too of any animal life. In fact the only sign of life was a pair of coyotes in the valley who had obviously found an interesting carcass, probably a jack rabbit, and were devouring it as quickly as they could tear it apart. One of the sly-looking animals glanced up at the figure on the top of the hill, then, having concluded that Cam didn't represent another meal, turned his attention back to the carcass.

Stagecoach to Damnation

Cam sat down and proceeded to light a cigar. He stared at the stage below and the passengers who were sitting around it. To his surprise one of them detached themselves from the others and began to slowly climb the hill. He saw that it was Doris Thompson.

He watched as she climbed the hill without any apparent effort. He concluded that she looked very attractive as she covered the last few yards and flopped down on the ground.

'You'll spoil your dress,' he informed her. 'It's pretty dusty up here.'

'It's all right, I'm a dressmaker,' she said, as she made herself comfortable by tucking her legs under her.

For several moments they stared in silence at the coyotes who were finishing off their meal. To Cam's surprise she said venomously, 'I hate those animals.'

'They're harmless. They won't attack humans. Not unless they're already dead.'

'I know. It's a stupid reaction. But I used to live on a lonely farm with my parents. I would hear them at night howling. I used to lay awake in my bed imagining what they would do to me if they caught me.' She shivered although the sun was at its height.

'Where was the farm?' asked Cam.

'I'll tell you when I get to know you better.' She

squinted at him through half-closed eyes. 'I don't suppose you ever lived on a lonely farm.'

'Sometimes.'

'And you're not going to tell me about it, either?'

'Not until I get to know you better.'

'You know sometimes you can be the most irritating person.' She stood up. 'I really came up here to tell you that the driver wants your help with the stage.'

Cam carefully ground out his cigar. They began to stride down the hill together. Gradually Doris began to increase the speed of her strides. 'Come on, I'll race you,' she said.

'You go on ahead,' said Cam.

She pouted. 'Don't you ever do anything on the spur of the moment?'

'Not very often,' said Cam.

Doris reached the others ahead of him to show him that she was annoyed with his last remark. The driver wanted Cam to help put the horses back in the shafts. When the task was completed the driver informed the passengers that they could get back inside the stage.

'There'll be a couple of places before we get to Herford where I'm afraid you'll have to get out and walk,' he said.

'As long as we get there in the end, that's the main thing,' said the reverend.

Stagecoach to Damnation

'We'll all owe you a whiskey,' said Bridges, ignoring Mrs Beeson's frown of disapproval.

7

The deputy sheriff, whose name was Phillips, made good time to reach the first staging post. He rode the horse at full gallop and arrived there just after midday. He swung the horse in a tight turn in front of the staging post.

He asked what time the stage had left and was informed by the old man that it was about three hours before. He changed horses and in ten minutes he was ready to resume his gallop. As he rode he mentally tried to calculate when he would catch the stage up. In about an hour and a half's time, he concluded.

The trail through the valley was deserted as he guessed it would be. He had only been to Herford two or three times but on each journey this valley had struck him as one of the most desolate in the territory. He involuntarily slowed his horse as he realized that if the horse should come across a

Stagecoach to Damnation

rattler or a sidewinder and stumble he would be alone in this wilderness.

He carried on at this steady pace for several miles. He reasoned that he would catch the stage long before it approached Herford. The only sign of life was a pair of ravens which were circulating idly overhead. He watched them to relieve the monotony of the ride. He realized too late that if he had been scanning the hillside instead of watching the ravens he might have become aware sooner of the presence of the Indian.

The Indian on top of the hill had quickly concluded that the approaching rider was travelling at the correct speed for him to get in a telling shot. If the rider had been galloping at full tilt he would not have been able to guarantee to kill him with one shot. But at this steady speed, the shot shouldn't prove to be any problem.

He shifted the Winchester until it settled comfortably into the crook of his shoulder. All he had to do was to wait until the rider came level with him. He noted that he had thick black hair. After he had shot him the hair would make an attractive scalp in his belt. It would take its place as one of his prize possessions – although of course it could never oust the tomahawk he had inherited from his father which had been used to dispatch at least half a dozen White Eyes in the battle of Little Big Horn.

The rider was almost level with him. His first shot would be vital. He wouldn't expect to get a second chance. If he missed, or only wounded him, the horse would bolt. He could now see the star on the rider's chest plainly. It was a perfect target.

He lined the sights up on the star. He took a deep breath as he had been taught. His finger was on the trigger and he was about to dispatch the rider to his god. Of course they say the White Eye's god was more powerful that the Indian god of the earth. For one thing the White Eye's god was really three gods in one and that *would* make him more powerful.

It was this thought which caused the Indian to fire a split second later than he should have. He saw the rider tumble from his saddle. He wasn't sure though whether he had succeeded in killing him.

In fact the deputy was still alive but with a burning pain in his shoulder which threatened to make him pass out at any minute. He still retained, though, enough of his senses to know that if he passed out the assassin on the hill would quickly descend to finish him off.

Luckily he had fallen off his horse near a sage-bush. Although it was only a couple of feet high its thick pale-green foliage gave him ample protection for the moment. His first priority was to try to stem the flow of blood from his shoulder. He realized that if he lost too much blood he would pass out.

He stuffed a handkerchief into the wound, almost crying with the pain as the handkerchief touched the raw flesh. He knew that the bullet was still inside and that unless it was taken out without too much delay blood-poisoning could set in. However that was something to attend to in the future. His present and only consideration at the moment was to kill the bastard who had tried to kill him. If he succeeded in doing that at least he would die a happy man. The only thing he could do at the moment was to wait and pray.

The Indian was undecided what to do. He couldn't see the rider because he was hidden by a sage-bush. Suppose the rider was still alive and able to use his gun. Surely the sensible thing to do was to ride away and leave him where he was. His horse, after bolting, was now peacefully grazing about a hundred yards away. The sensible thing to do was to shoot the horse and then even if the rider was still alive he wouldn't be able to escape from this valley. Not unless he walked all the way to Herford.

Yes, that seemed the sensible thing to do. He levelled his gun. The deputy heard the shot and saw the horse slowly collapse. The bastard – he had shot his horse. Not that he had any particular feelings for the horse – his horse was in the staging-post where he had changed it. But it was obvious that the bastard was determined that he would die one way or another in this hell of a valley. It strengthened his determination to stay alive at all costs.

Now the sensible thing to do was to ride away. Leave the lawman to his fate. Let the coyotes and ravens eat his flesh. There was no way he could escape from this desolate place, assuming he was still alive. Probably the next visitors to the valley would be the next stage and that would be a week into the future.

There was only one thing which prevented him riding away – the scalp. It was a perfect scalp with its thick black hair. He licked his lips. He knew he would suffer a thousand tortures if he rode away without cutting off that scalp.

The chances were the rider was dead anyhow. He had only held back his shot for a split second. His bullet could still have found the driver's heart. He knew that he would never sleep again if he did not have that scalp.

All he had to do was to go down carefully with his Winchester at the ready. If the rider were still alive he would finish him off. Then there would be the delicious moment when he would cut the skin across the rider's forehead to begin a clean removal of the scalp. It would have to be a clean cut since he would want nothing to spoil the perfection of the prize which he would take home to his beloved Little Moonbeam. He began to ride slowly down the hillside.

Phillips heard the horse descending the hillside. That was the first mistake the killer had made. If he had walked down the hillside it was likely that he wouldn't have heard him. But the horse slithering down the slope had told him that the gunman was on his way. Well, he was ready for him. Or at least as ready as he ever would be in his wounded condition.

The Indian knew the sage-bush under which the rider had crawled. More than likely he had crawled there to die the way some animals crawl into a hole or cave to spend their last moments hidden away from prying eyes. It was a natural thing for animals to do – to seek their last moments of privacy before dying.

The lawman was right underneath the bush so that it was almost difficult to see him. The Indian considered blasting a few shots into him to make sure that he was dead. That could have the disadvantage of blood splattering all over the place and spoiling his prize of the beautiful scalp. He mentally savoured their love-making after Little Moonbeam had accepted the beautiful scalp. He approached cautiously.

The lawman was so still that he decided he had

nothing to fear. He drew up his horse when he was a few yards away. He slipped off the horse but in doing so for a moment his rifle wasn't aiming at the deputy. In that brief moment Phillips swung round even though the pain was excruciating and shot the Indian whose father had aptly christened him Not-Right-in-the-Head. Surprise registered on his face as he tried to swing his rifle round to let fly a bullet of his own. But Phillips with his Colt was quicker. He poured all his bullets into the Indian. Now I can die a happy man, he thought, before passing out.

8

Ed Smith was so successful at making his whiskey that he sold out the first consignment in less than an hour. 'If I had known it was going to be as successful as this I would have started ages ago,' he said.

'You should have charged five dollars a bottle,' said Harriet.

With the first three dollars Ed bought a flashy tie-pin for himself and a pink ribbon for his daughter. After admiring himself in the mirror he told Harriet, 'It will take us ten days to make more whiskey.'

'The still isn't big enough,' stated Harriet positively.

'I know. I've tried Hardcastle the ironmonger, but he says it will take him weeks to get a larger still. He suggested that I should try Stoneville. There's a large ironmonger's store there owned by a Mr Collins. In fact he sent a telegram to him to ask if he had a bigger still. Collins sent a telegram back saying yes, he has.'

'It's unusual for him to send you to somebody else for something he could supply in a few weeks' time, isn't it?' asked Harriet.

'He bought three bottles of my whiskey.'

'That figures,' she retorted.

That was why the following morning Ed and Harriet set out with their wagon to Stoneville. Harriet was secretly delighted at their journey. Anything was better than trying to persuade some of the folk in Herford that she was an innocent bystander listening to Ed's spiel and being persuaded to buy some of his balsam. They had 'worked' a dozen towns like Herford in the territory and each time after a few weeks a man with a star would appear on the outskirts of the crowd. He would wait quietly until she had made her appearance and a few bottles had been sold. He would approach her father and say that they had twenty-four hours to leave the town or end up in jail for obtaining money by deceit. Ed knew it was not worth arguing. They invariably left the town early the following morning.

Now, however, there was a chance of a whole new life. If they could get a larger still and, say, they could sell fifty bottles instead of a dozen each time they could soon build up a nice nest-egg. She might soon be able to buy a new dress to go with the ribbon her father had bought.

They came across the stage a short while after it had been repaired and was making slow progress along the trail. Ed drew to one side to let it pass. To his surprise the driver reined in his horses.

'Keep your eyes peeled for an Indian wearing war paint,' said Lawson.

'Has he attacked the stage?' asked a shocked Ed.

'No, but he followed it for a couple of miles until one of one of our passengers got too trigger-happy and shot at him.'

'What happened?' asked Harriet.

'He scared the Indian, but the shot also scared the horses. They bolted. That's why we're crawling into Herford.'

'I'll keep a look-out for the Indian,' promised a worried Ed.

The meeting with the stage meant that the rest of the journey for Harriet was less enjoyable than it had been. They both kept scanning the horizon for the Indian. Due to the fact that they were busy watching the tops of the hills they came upon the figure lying on the ground almost before they realized it.

'It's the Indian,' said Ed, unnecessarily.

Stagecoach to Damnation

Most of the deputy's bullets had ended up in the Indian's body, which was now a gory mass of entrails and splintered bone. They had jumped down from the wagon and Ed, reasoning that the Indian's Winchester would be no use to him now, tossed it into the wagon. Harriet, who was busy being sick, was holding on to the wagon for support when she realized there was somebody under the nearby sage-bush. She pointed him out to her father.

'Is he dead, too?' she asked, fearfully.

'No, but he's not far off it,' replied Ed. After completing his examination, he straightened. 'He's got a bullet in his shoulder. We've got to get that wound cleaned up before poisoning sets in. We might even be too late as it is.'

'We could clean him up with the water in our canteens,' suggested Harriet.

'No, it might start the bleeding again. The best thing we can do is to get him to the next stage-post. Maybe he can stay there. When we get to Stoneville we'll tell a doctor about him.'

They carried him carefully on to the wagon. To their relief the bleeding didn't start again. Ed put a clean piece of linen where the deputy had stuffed his handkerchief. He looked around for something to keep the plug in its place. There was nothing obviously available on the wagon. Harriet sighed and took out the new ribbon from her hair. He smiled at her as he accepted it. 'You're a good kid, Harriet,' he informed her.

'I know,' she replied, resignedly.

9

They reached the staging post without the deputy starting to bleed again. Ed explained to the old couple that the deputy had been shot. He added that if he could leave him there he would be going to Stoneville where he would find a doctor and send him back to take care of the deputy.

The couple protested that they were too old to take care of a wounded man. Couldn't he take the deputy all the way to Stoneville? Ed pointed out that the ride would probably start the deputy bleeding again, in which case he might not reach Stoneville alive. At this point Harriet stepped in and volunteered to stay at the staging-post to look after the deputy. The old couple sighed with relief at that solution to the problem.

'You're a good kid, Harriet,' said Ed.

She watched her father set off in the wagon.

Stagecoach to Damnation

The deputy was still unconscious so she accepted the old woman's offer of hot biscuits and coffee.

Ed continued on his monotonous progress to Stoneville, the journey now made even more boring by the fact that Harriet was no longer present to chatter to him. He wondered what the Indian had been doing shooting at the deputy. It was obvious from the way he had found the bodies and then the dead horse that the Indian had shot at them both, with slightly less success with the deputy than the horse. He knew that Indians no longer shot at white men – and had stopped doing so several years before when the Indian Wars had ended. Of course there were roaming bands of Indians up north near Damnation who still ignored the cease-fire and who carried on with the traditional Indian pastimes of descending on isolated farms, and killing and scalping the White Eyes. However the present attempt at a killing was very puzzling; still it managed to occupy his attention as the wagon slowly ate up the miles to Stoneville.

When he reached the town he explained the whole situation to the fat sheriff.

'So you say my deputy is at the staging-post,' said the sheriff, while he mentally digested the whole picture.

'That's right. My daughter, Harriet, is taking care of him.'

Stagecoach to Damnation

'You'd better get the doctor to visit him. He lives at the far end of Main Street, past the Red Garter saloon.'

Ed privately thought that the sheriff might have been concerned enough about his deputy and therefore would arrange to see the doctor himself. However he left the office and headed for the doctor's house. The doctor, a stocky ginger-haired man, agreed to ride out and examine the deputy.

In the staging post Harriet had been hoping and praying that the deputy wouldn't recover until the doctor arrived. She knew nothing about nursing a wounded man and realized that the old couple would be of very little help to her.

She was sitting by his bed and glancing at him fearfully from time to time in case there was any sign of recovery when the old lady came in. 'We usually have dinner at this time,' she said. 'I'm afraid it's only rabbit stew, but you're welcome to join us if you wish.'

Harriet thankfully accepted the invitation. They were half-way through the meal when they heard a loud groan from the bedroom. Harriet jumped up and rushed to the deputy's side. He appeared to be conscious but his eyes didn't seem to be focusing on anything as he twisted and turned in his bed. To Harriet's relief there was no sign of any further bleeding.

Stagecoach to Damnation

'He's delirious,' said the old woman, who had followed Harriet into the bedroom. 'The only thing you can do is to cool him down by putting plenty of cold compresses on his forehead. I'll get you a bowl of water and some cloths.'

For the next hour or so Harriet put compress after compress on the deputy's feverish brow. He twisted and turned in the bed uttering names with which Harriet was not familiar and making unintelligible remarks. Among the names one stood out – Esme. Harriet wondered who she was – maybe his girlfriend. Probably not his wife since she assumed he wasn't married because he wasn't wearing a wedding-ring.

In the hours before the doctor arrived Harriet must have smoothed the deputy's brow a hundred times. His thick hair was soaked with a mixture of perspiration and the attention of Harriet's cloths. It was dark when the doctor arrived. He went straight to see the deputy without any preamble. He examined the wound while Harriet watched fearfully.

'I've got to get the bullet out,' he announced. Harriet watched while he performed the operation. She surprised herself by not fainting when she saw the doctor holding the bullet in his tweezers. 'He was lucky. The bullet didn't touch the bone. Of course he'll have to stay like this until the fever subsides.'

'How long will that be?' asked Harriet.

The doctor shrugged. 'It's hard to tell. Could be two days; could be two weeks. Anyhow I'll leave some medicine. When he recovers give it to him twice a day – at morning and night. Now I'll clean up the wound. Have you got a bed where I can stay the rest of the night?' He addressed the last remark to the old woman who was standing nearby.

'Yes, Doctor,' she replied.

'I assume you'll be looking after him,' the doctor addressed Harriet.

'I haven't got much choice, have I?' she exclaimed.

10

It was dark too when the stage finally arrived in Herford. Apart from the increasing number of questions which Lawson and Cam received from the passengers about what time the stage would eventually arrive, there were no repercussions from the broken spindle. The general feeling was of relief that they had arrived safely in Herford, everything considered.

They had all been booked in at the Bull Hotel. 'You don't have to get up early,' Lawson informed them. 'You've got a free day tomorrow. We aren't due to start on the last stage until the following day. We'll have the broken spindle fixed by then,' he added.

The following morning one of the early risers was Leonard Bridges. He refused the offer of breakfast, having only a cup of coffee before setting out briskly from the hotel and heading for

Stagecoach to Damnation

the High Street. His obvious desire to reach his destination as quickly as possible helped to make him oblivious to the person who was following him. If in fact he had turned round and caught a glimpse of the person who was trailing him he would instantly have recognized him as one of his fellow travellers on the stage – the one who had fired the shot at the Indian, Clay Sterne.

Bridges reached his destination within five minutes – it was a bank. Even at this early hour it was open, the manager's slogan being that it was the early bank that catches the customer. Bridges, having disclosed his name was immediately ushered into the manager's office.

The manager, a tall, ginger-headed Scotsman named McCloud, having shaken hands with his visitor and offered him a cup of coffee which Bridges politely refused, said, 'Let's get down to business, Mr Bridges.'

'I'm ready, Mr McCloud,' said Bridges, rubbing his hands together in eager anticipation of their agreement.

McCloud, who was ultra-cautious, went to his office door. He opened it swiftly to make sure that nobody was eavesdropping. Satisfied, he returned to his seat. 'You can't be too careful,' he informed Bridges.

'I agree,' said Bridges. After all, the arrangement involved a lot of money – fifty thousand dollars in fact. Many people had been known to commit murder for a hundredth of that amount, and even considerably less.

'The arrangements are in hand,' said McCloud.

'Good,' said Bridges, rubbing his hands again. He knew it was a habit which irritated his wife. He had picked it up when he had first gone into banking as a young man thirty years before, and somehow it had stuck with him ever since.

'Two of my staff have already gone on ahead to Damnation,' said McCloud. 'They are ready to open the bank when the consignment of money arrives. Of course we haven't been able to announce in advance exactly when the bank will open. We must keep that a secret. Security is our watchword.'

'Exactly,' said Bridges. This time, by a conscious effort, he was able to refrain from rubbing his hands.

'The wagon containing the money will set off before the bank has opened tomorrow,' McCloud continued. 'That means that you should arrive in Damnation at roughly the same time as the wagon. Unfortunately the telegraph hasn't yet reached Damnation so there's no way I can tell them that you are coming. But the two men on the wagon are reliable men and they will help you to set everything up. In addition of course there are the two men who are already in Damnation.'

Stagecoach to Damnation

'Will there be any guards on the wagon?' asked Bridges.

'No, I don't think it will be necessary. Just one riding shotgun. I've used this method of transferring money before and it has worked with other branches,' McCloud reassured him.

'As long as you think it's safe and nobody will get hurt,' said Bridges.

'Are you sure you won't have a cup of coffee now?' asked McCloud.

'Why not?' replied the other. 'Everything seems to have been satisfactorily arranged.'

11

Bridges might not have been so complacent if he had seen another meeting which took place during the lunch hour in the Star Hotel a couple of hundred yards from the bank. There were three men sitting at a corner table. One was Clay Sterne, the other was a well-dressed young man wearing a dark suit with a flower in his buttonhole who might have worked in a men's outfitter's shop, but who was in fact an employee in the bank that Bridges had left three hours before. His name was Melton. The third was a tough looking character who looked as though he chewed nails named Wakely.

'All right, what can you tell us?' Sterne addressed the remark to Melton.

'You realize of course that if it came out that I gave you this information I could end up in jail

Stagecoach to Damnation

for years,' said Melton, who was showing signs of becoming anxious.

'Tell us what we want to know or I'll break your arm,' said Wakely conversationally as though he had just passed an observation about the weather.

Melton paled. For the first time he fully realized what he was getting into by passing the information on to these two crooks. It was obvious though that he now had no choice but to go through with it.

'There'll be a wagon leaving the bank tomorrow. It'll be setting off early carrying the money to start a new bank in Damnation.'

'How many men will be on it?' demanded Wakely.

'Two. One of them is named Peter Giles. He's the one who gave me the information.'

'A friend of yours?' asked Wakely, with a sneer.

'He's my brother-in-law,' answered Melton, shortly. 'He'll expect some payment when you get the money.'

'He'll get his cut,' said Sterne smoothly.

'And you'll get yours,' added Wakely.

Melton wondered whether there was any hidden sinister meaning in those words as he glanced at Wakely's hard face. Aloud he said: 'You don't want me here any longer, do you?'

'No, you've told us all we wanted to know,' said

Stagecoach to Damnation

Sterne, with a friendly smile.

'Now you can hop it,' said Wakely.

The two watched him as he made a hurried escape. 'So all we have to do is to hold up the wagon when it's on its way to Damnation,' stated Sterne. 'If there are two men on board it will take three men to make sure we kill them,' he added, as though he were doing a simple arithmetic sum in a classroom.

'I've already arranged it. They're in town waiting for me to get in touch with them.'

'Have you fixed a place where the ambush will take place?'

'Of course I have,' snapped Wakely.

Sterne realized that he was treading on thin ice. Wakely in a good mood was somebody to be feared, but when he was in a bad temper he was completely unpredictable. He had known Wakely to kill a man just because he hadn't invited him into his house when Wakely had called to collect a debt which the unfortunate person owed to a local store.

'Good,' replied Sterne.

'It's a deserted valley about six miles out of town,' supplied the other.

'Then after you've taken the wagon with the money the three of you meet me in Damnation. We share out the money and from there we'll go our separate ways. We're not far from the

Canadian border. It might be worthwhile slipping over the border.'

'I've got my own plans,' snapped Wakely. 'Nobody's going to tell me where to go.'

'Of course not,' said Sterne, hurriedly. He paused as he came to the hardest part of the meeting. He knew he would have to pluck up enough courage to say it, but it wasn't easy. 'If you should try to double-cross me, I've left all the details of the robbery with a solicitor. They're to be opened if I should be killed or disappear. There's enough evidence in there to send you to jail for the rest of your life.'

'You seem to have thought of everything don't you?' sneered Wakely.

'I think so,' said Sterne, having breathed a heavy sign of relief at having got his speech out of the way. 'I'll see you in Damnation then,' he added.

'If not I'll see you in hell,' said Wakely.

Sterne wondered what exactly he meant by that as he watched his companion in crime slowly leave the saloon.

12

Later in the afternoon Doris Thompson was strolling in the high street looking at the shop-windows. She stopped outside a dressmaker's and gazed at the variety of dresses and hats in the window.

'Wishful thinking?' asked Cam, who had approached without her realizing it.

'I feel like a girl looking at a sweet-shop knowing I can't afford any,' she explained.

'You'll be all right in Damnation,' said Cam. 'People there won't be expecting to buy dresses at these prices.'

She swung round to face him. 'Have you noticed anything about me today?' she demanded.

He studied her. 'Only that you're your usual attractive self.'

Her eyes flashed angrily. 'I'm talking about the dress I'm wearing.'

'I'd say it looks very attractive – if I may say so,' he added hastily after seeing the way her lips tightened warningly.

'It's the same dress that I've been wearing for the last three days,' she said, icily.

'Even though you're a dressmaker...' He paused in puzzlement.

'I mean I couldn't change my dress this morning like the preacher's wife because my dresses are all on top of the stage as luggage. I'm only allowed to bring twenty-five pounds in weight with me. All my stock of cloth and six dresses are up there, I'll have a sewing-machine sent on with the next stage.'

'I don't see what you're worrying about,' said Cam. 'Nothing's going to happen to the stage.'

'I wish I was as confident as you. I stayed up half the night worrying about what would happen if I lost all my stock.'

'It'll be all right,' Cam stated, trying to reassure her.

'What about that Indian? What if there are more of his sort around?'

'There was nothing to be afraid of from him. He was acting on his own.'

'How do you know that?' She glanced at him keenly.

'If there had been others they would have attacked the stage before it reached Herford,' he explained.

'How do you know he hasn't ridden on ahead and joined his companions who are waiting for us the other side of Herford?'

'I don't. But it doesn't seem likely.'

'I wish I had the same faith in your crystal ball as you have,' she retorted.

'Come on,' he said, 'I'll buy you a cup of coffee.'

There was a coffee-house next door. She hesitated for a moment then smiled sweetly at him. 'All right,' she concurred.

When they were seated at the table the conversation naturally turned to the other travellers on the stage.

'I've been wondering about Sam Melrose,' she stated. 'I've been trying to guess why he's going to Damnation. It helps to pass the time away on the stage,' she added.

'I can tell you,' said Cam, as he sipped his coffee.

'I think I've finally worked it out too,' she said.

'All right, what's your guess?'

'In the first place he's not a cowboy; judging by his hands he's never done any hard work. Am I right so far?'

'Correct.'

'And he's too young to be anybody of importance. Also he doesn't talk like a teacher. Therefore I'd say he's going to Damnation to work in a saloon. As a barman,' she concluded triumphantly.

'You're half-way right.'

'What do you mean, half-way?' she said, a doubtful tone having crept into her voice.

'He *is* going to work in a saloon. But in front of the bar, not behind it.'

'You mean as' – she groped for the word then finally produced it like a conjurer producing a rabbit out of a hat – 'gambler.'

'That's it.'

'How do you know?'

'He told me.'

'Do you know you can be very irritating at times,' she said, pretending annoyance. She thought for a moment then added doubtfully, 'He looks a bit young.'

'They come at all ages. I started gambling when I was five. My elder brother and I would toss a coin to see whether it was heads or tails. He always won. I found out later that it was a double-headed coin.'

'That was one of your first lessons in life?'

'Yeah. After I'd beaten my brother up I never gambled again.'

Their conversation which had started off as casual banter seemed to have taken a serious turn, Doris noted, as she watched Cam staring out through the window. Perhaps he was seeing a young boy learning another lesson in that the older brother whom he had been looking up to until that moment in the past had turned out to be somebody he couldn't trust, and who had feet of clay.

13

All that afternoon in the bank Melton's thoughts kept returning to his lunch-time conversation with Wakely. The man scared him as he never believed a human being could. In fact his thoughts were distracting him so much from his work that on two occasions he gave a customer the wrong change. On both occasions the customer noticed the mistake and was able to correct the error before it was brought to the attention of McCloud, who was seated on his high stool in the inner office.

What had he done? Mellon racked his brains feverishly for a way out of the terrible mess he was in. He tried to concentrate on the positive side of the situation – the five thousand dollars he would receive for divulging the information about the shipment of money to Damnation. The money would be used to help to relieve his mother's pain. She was dying of cancer and the only thing which could help her was a regular supply of laudanum. Unfortunately it was very costly. In order to pay for it he had had to become involved with the crooks.

Try to think of something positive. Perhaps it wouldn't be so bad after all. Once the crooks had taken the money there wouldn't be anything to connect him with the theft. After all it was the bank's money. It didn't belong to any personal member of the bank. It wasn't as if he was helping to steal from a member of the public. The money would be replaced by one of the big insurance companies. In a couple of months' time the whole affair would be forgotten. Wakely would be far enough away. Probably spending his money among the fleshpots in San Francisco. No, perhaps things wouldn't be too bad after all.

He'd have enough money to give his mother a good vacation before she passed away. She'd always wanted to go to St Louis – maybe when he'd received the money he would be able to take her there. The snag was she was astute enough to realize that he would not be able to take her on a holiday like that without its costing a few hundred dollars. Perhaps he could say he had won it by gambling. No, she'd never swallow that since she knew he was not a gambler. Anyhow she would never accept any money which had come as a result of gambling since she was a devout churchgoer. Also the long journey by stage and then train could be too painful for her. No, he'd better forget about that idea and just think about relieving her suffering for the last six months the doctor had given her.

Six o'clock couldn't come quickly enough. The last hour from five o'clock dragged past more slowly than he had ever known it to. Mr McCloud, as if he felt that time was dragging too, came out to the front of the bank several times during the last hour. It was unusual for him to do this since he usually contented himself with coming out only once or twice to make sure that everything was in smooth running order. Or did he suspect that something was wrong? Melton broke out into an instant sweat at the thought.

Six o'clock finally came and Melton stepped outside the bank. He set off down the high street, never looking round. He wanted to get home as quickly as possible. He wanted to get away from the bank – which had suddenly assumed an unknown threatening quality. He had always liked the building up to that moment. It had always had a nice friendly aura about it. As far as its architecture was concerned it did not stand out in the high street like the church or the town hall. But it was a solid, dependable building. The sort of building that people could trust. But not any more. Because now there was a snake inside the building. The snake being himself.

He had about a mile to walk before reaching their house. On the way several people – mostly women – acknowledged him as he passed. He was a presentable young man – always smartly dressed. One day he would make somebody's daughter a nice, smart husband, although today he seemed rather preoccupied. In fact he did not return their greeting. That in itself was rather unusual, since he was always a polite young man.

He entered the house.

'Hullo, dear, is that you?' said his mother from the kitchen.

He went through to kiss her on the cheek as he had always done. She was putting the finishing touches to the stew that they would have for dinner. He couldn't help reflecting that with the money he would receive from the robbery he would be able to buy a larger variety of food than they had at the moment.

There was a knock at the door. He went back out through the sitting-room to answer it. To his horror it was Wakely. He was carrying a rifle under his arm. At the sight of the accursed man his knees almost buckled under him. 'What – what do you want?' he managed to stammer out.

'I'm just making sure that you didn't tell anyone in the bank about our little arrangement,' said Wakely with a smile as friendly as a wolf's.

'Of course I didn't. Do you take me for a fool,' he gasped.

'I was just making sure,' said Wakely. With that he reversed the rifle and hit Melton full in the face with the butt. The blow was so unexpected that Melton made no effort to avoid it. He collapsed in a mess of blood. Even lying on the floor in excruciating pain his one thought was that he wouldn't call out for help since he wouldn't want his mother to see him in such a terrible condition. Wakely took full advantage of Melton's silence by hitting him several times in the head. With the second blow Melton lost consciousness. He died with the fifth.

His mother, who was rather deaf, eventually realized that something was amiss and came out to investigate. She had the presence of mind to bring out the red-hot poker from the fire. When she saw her son's bloodied body on the floor and Wakely standing over it she let out a god-almighty scream. Wakely advanced quickly to try to silence her before her screams brought the neighbours to investigate. She hesitated for a moment with the ridiculous thought that the only thing she wanted to do was somehow to cover her son's mangled body so that nobody else could see the disfigurement of his face. Wakely seized the moment to deliver a telling blow to her head. She staggered, but before she fell she flailed out with the red-hot poker. The instrument caught Wakely across the side of his face causing him to yell with pain. She would never know it but her last involuntary movement had caused a scar which Wakely would carry with him for the rest of his life.

Having satisfied himself that she too was dead, Wakely stepped inside the house and shut the door. He wondered whether any of the neighbours had heard the scream. After a few minutes when there was no sign of anyone rushing to investigate he began to relax.

He went into the kitchen where the fire was burning brightly. He poured some cold water on to a cloth and dabbed it on his face to try to ease the pain. His next move was to go upstairs. There were two bedrooms. He chose the largest. He went over to the bed and pulled the bedclothes off the bed. The mattress followed and he staggered with it downstairs. Back in the kitchen he found an old newspaper. He rolled it up and, putting it in the fire, he lit it. When it was burning to his satisfaction he applied it to the mattress. Soon that too was burning merrily.

He left by the back door knowing that the timber-framed house would burn to the ground in a remarkably short time.

14

The following morning there were two meetings in Herford. The first was held in the lounge of the Bull Hotel. The travellers on the stage had gathered there at the request of the driver, Lawson. Having made sure that they were all present, he began his announcement.

'I'm sorry but the stage will not be leaving today.'

There was puzzlement and consternation on the faces of the seven listeners. 'The reason,' he continued, with his voice choked with emotion, 'is that my sister, Mrs Melton, and her son were killed last night.'

They waited for him to continue. He took a deep breath. 'While you were having breakfast the deputy sheriff came to inform me that they had burned to death in their house last night.'

'Oh, no!' There was a gasp of horror from the listeners.

Stagecoach to Damnation

He had been standing to make the announcement but now, as if his legs had given way under him, he sat down abruptly.

'What happened?' asked Cam, who was standing near him.

'We don't know yet. She lived in one of those wooden-framed houses on the edge of town. Once the flames had caught it went up in minutes. The neighbours tried to put out the flames, but they were beaten back. In the end they were lucky to save their own properties.'

'Is there anything we can do?' asked the reverend.

'No, thanks,' said Lawson, having partly recovered his composure.

Doris moved over to him and put her hand on his shoulder. 'Don't worry,' she said. 'We realize you can't leave now. You'll have to stay here for the funeral. Just let us know when you will eventually be able to leave here.'

Her remarks were echoed by the others. 'We realize we'll have to stay here a few days extra,' said Mrs Beeson, 'but it's not the end of the world. You make all the family arrangements you have to make. We'll all be on hand should you need any of us. Especially my husband.'

Lawson was visibly moved by the signs of sympathetic solidarity of the group. 'Thanks,' he said. 'And I'm sure that if my sister were alive

Stagecoach to Damnation

now she would also thank you for your support.' He got up and left the room quickly.

The group broke up with very little conversation. 'What a terrible way to die,' Doris confided to Cam as they left the room.

'Yeah,' said Cam. 'It makes you realize that life doesn't go on for ever,' he added, enigmatically.

The one person whose reaction was totally at odds with the others, although he couldn't show it, was Sterne. He went straight to his room after Lawson's announcement, not pausing to speak to anyone. He poured himself a stiff whiskey.

What was Wakely thinking about? For there was no doubt in his mind that Wakely was behind the burning of Melton and his mother. It was too much of a co-incidence to think that a few hours after their meeting with Melton the fire had been an accident.

Why had Wakely done it? The obvious explanation was that Wakely was mad. He had already concluded that, and if it wasn't for the fact that Wakely was indispensable, with his local knowledge and contacts, to steal the money that was being transferred to the bank in Damnation he would never have gone within a mile of him. But he had thought that Wakely would go along with their original plan which was to give Melton five thousand dollars for keeping quiet about his part in the robbery.

Stagecoach to Damnation

Why had Wakely done it? The question kept coming back to him. He took another stiff whiskey to try to subdue the recurring question. Was there another reason apart from Wakely's obvious madness? Had Wakely found out that Melton had informed the bank-manager about the whole plan? Sterne's blood ran cold at the thought.

No, surely not; he corrected the idea quickly. If Melton had revealed Wakely's name and his own then surely the bank-manager would have contacted the sheriff yesterday. This would have inevitably led to the sheriff and his deputy showing up at the hotel with an invitation for him to accompany them to the jail. No, the fact that they had not come to question him showed that the law so far had no idea about the robbery.

So it came back to the theory that Wakely had killed Melton because he was mad. Unless of course he wanted to silence Melton because there was a slight possibility that Melton would crack under cross-questioning after the robbery had been completed. Yes, that made sense. Perhaps Wakely had been thinking ahead, and had eliminated one of the possibilities of a slip-up to their plans. Yes, maybe Wakely wasn't *entirely* mad. Sterne poured himself another drink. Maybe things would turn out all right after all.

The second meeting was held in the sheriff's

office. Apart from the sheriff and his deputy, McCloud was also present. The sheriff had expressed his sympathy about the Meltons' deaths and his deputy had concurred.

The sheriff, named Dryden, was a middle-aged stocky man who had once been a farmer but had given up that physically demanding occupation to keep the law in Herford. It was widely rumoured that although he had given up horse-breeding he hadn't given up his appreciation of fillies as his regular dalliance with some of the attractive widows in the town showed. His deputy, named Gill, was a thin, academic young man who spent most of his spare time immersed in his books. His ambition was to become a lawyer and the constant studying by lamplight and candlelight had already affected his eyesight to the point where he was forced to wear glasses to read, although on duty he didn't wear them in the office lest they would destroy the image he was trying to cultivate of a tough lawman.

'The question is – was it an accident?' said the sheriff, thoughtfully.

'What else could it have been?' asked McCloud.

'I remember when I had my farm there was a mystery fire at a farm nearby. It was burnt to the ground like the Meltons' house. So there was no evidence regarding what happened. However the daughter had rejected a local boy who had come courting her. And the general opinion was that he burnt the house down in a fit of rage.'

'There was no boyfriend involved with the Meltons' house,' Gill pointed out reasonably.

'I know,' replied the other. 'But the point is somebody could have started the fire deliberately. I don't suppose we'll ever find out the truth though.'

'One of the neighbours seems to think that Mrs Melton fell into the fire while she was cooking her son's dinner,' said McCloud. 'She was ill, suffering from cancer. The doctor used to give her laudanum and this used to make her kind of dopey. The neighbour says that sometimes she didn't know rightly what she was doing. If she fell in the fire and her son tried to save her, then they could both have caught fire.'

'Yeah, I suppose it could have happened that way,' said the sheriff, scratching a thoughtful chin.

'On the other hand perhaps there is something suspicious about their deaths,' pursued McCloud, leaning back in his chair contemplating the ceiling. 'It does seem a bit of a coincidence that yesterday one of the bank employees died and this morning we'll be sending a consignment of money to start a bank in Damnation.'

'How many men have you got going with the wagon?' asked the sheriff.

Stagecoach to Damnation

'Two.'

'Then may I suggest taking a third?' said the sheriff. 'He won't ride in sight, but he'll be hidden under a tarpaulin. If there is a robbery and the two on the wagon are killed, the third one will appear when the tarpaulin is pulled back. He'll have the element of surprise on his side. He should be able to kill the robbers.'

'Where am I going to get someone at short notice?' asked McCloud. 'The consignment is due to be loaded in an hour.'

Dryden stared across at Gill. It was the sort of stare that made his deputy's stomach turn over. 'You've always fancied some action,' he said. 'Now's your chance.'

McCloud looked doubtful. 'Are you sure you're up to it, son?' he demanded.

Gill almost swallowed his Adam's apple before replying. 'Sure.' He sounded confident, though inwardly he was trembling like a leaf.

'Good,' said McCloud. 'In that case you'd better come over to the bank with me and we'll make the final arrangements.'

Gill wondered whether there was anything significant in McCloud's choice of the word 'final', as he prepared to accompany the bank manager.

15

Wakely waited by Trasker's Canyon with his rifle at the ready. He had chosen a vantage point near the mouth of the canyon where he would spot the wagon about a mile before it entered the canyon. Once inside there would be no shelter for the wagon as it moved slowly along the floor of the canyon. The two carrying the money would be sitting ducks for his bullets.

The only slight doubt in his mind was whether the bank-manager, McCloud, would keep to his original plan of moving the money that day. Maybe out of respect for his dead employee McCloud would halt the movement of the money, say until after the funeral. Wakely chewed on some tobacco as he considered the problem.

There was no way he would know if there had been a change of plan – no way that is, unless he stayed here till sundown. If the wagon hadn't

Stagecoach to Damnation

appeared by then he could assume that it wasn't going to come that day. He spat at a grasshopper to show his dislike of the idea.

The doubt about the delivery had come about because he'd killed Melton, but he hadn't had any choice. Melton was the sort of yellow-livered rat who would go crawling to his boss and confess the whole thing. He knew that sort. He'd met them before. He'd had a lot of dealings with them when he was boss of his own gang. And he'd left a lot of corpses behind as evidence of the way he'd dealt with them. He couldn't stand deceit. He liked everything to be open and above-board. Life was complicated enough without some clever bastard trying to tie it up into knots. He liked everything to be simple, and he intended to keep it that way.

He shifted the rifle slightly from its position. What was he thinking about – of course he wouldn't have to wait until sundown. If McCloud decided to move the money today then the wagon would start that morning. They would want to get as many miles behind them as they could during the day. Which meant that the wagon would arrive probably before high noon. He squinted at the sun to try to fix its position – it looked pretty high in the sky to him. It was at times like this that he wished he had learnt to tell the time.

How much money had Sterne said would be in

the wagon? He had said $100,000. He couldn't even begin to picture such an amount. The most money he had ever seen was at a card table where the gamblers had built up a pot of $2,000. Everyone in the saloon had stopped what they were doing to watch the game. When one of the players had called everybody had held their breath. He finally won with four jacks. That was $2,000. It was a lot of money. More than he had ever earned. But it was chicken-feed to what he would be getting when he held up the wagon.

Was it going to come today? What was holding it up? He squinted into the distance, but there was no sign of it. He knew that when it did come he would have to be accurate with his shots. He had to kill the person riding shot-gun with his first shot. This would leave the driver, who would be too busy trying to control the horses to fire a shot at him. This should give him plenty of time to take aim and kill him too. Then it would just be a matter of riding down to the wagon, collecting the money and putting it in his saddle-bag. He licked his lips in eager anticipation of the event.

Suddenly it was there! One minute he had been staring into the distance at an empty landscape, then the next minute there it was. The wagon was approaching in a cloud of dust which suggested that it was being driven quickly.

Stagecoach to Damnation

Possibly the driver was making up for lost time. Well, if he knew what was going to happen to him he'd slow down and enjoy his last few minutes on Earth. Wakely's face spread into a thin smile at the thought.

As the wagon drew nearer he could see the two men on the buckboard more clearly. He couldn't distinguish their faces, but that didn't matter. He knew that the shotgun would be on his side, and as the wagon slowed to come round the awkward bend about 200 yards away – that would be his chance. One shot in the heart, then quickly line up for the second shot. He felt the familiar thrill of a prospective kill as he waited for the stage to come nearer.

Gill was lying under the tarpaulin. Normally he was not a praying man. He was an avid reader on most subjects and the more he read the less he found himself believing in God. After all they were living in a scientific age. Progress was everywhere. The telegraph was rapidly spreading to the four corners of the United States. Railroads were opening up even the remotest territories. Who knew what the next century would bring in a dozen years' time? Yet, at times like this, when you were lying concealed and sweating under a tarpaulin a belief in God would be a very convenient thing to have claim to.

Everything was going to be all right, wasn't it?

Stagecoach to Damnation

Surely nobody was going to attack the wagon. They would arrive safely in Damnation, wouldn't they? *Our Father, which art in heaven....*

Wakely lined up the shot. He always liked to count when he was about to shoot someone like this. He found that it helped his concentration. Not that he could count to more than a dozen, but then he'd never need to count as far as that with a simple shot like this. *One* ... he automatically exhaled. *Two* ... he stared unblinkingly at the target. *Three* ... the target was almost near enough. *Four* ... he had the familiar feeling of being in absolute control. *Five* ... Fire!

The man riding shot-gun was hit squarely in the chest. He toppled from the wagon without a murmur. Under the tarpaulin Gill emptied his bladder. At the sound of the second shot he almost pushed the cover away to find out what was going on. Naked fear restrained him.

Wakely was congratulating himself on how easy the whole thing had been. They were probably two of the best shots he had ever fired. Both plumb in the heart. Neither man knew what had hit him. The horses hadn't even bolted. True, the startled horses were both pawing the ground as if they were undecided what to do next. So he'd better get down there quickly and get hold of the reins before they realized there was nobody in control and they could make a dash for freedom.

Stagecoach to Damnation

Barely two minutes had passed before he approached the horses carefully. He was unconcerned about the two bodies which were lying on the trail. He talked to the horses as he approached them. He was always good with horses, having realized at an early age that they were more likely to respond favourably if you talked to them in a calm voice first. The black roan was beginning to show every sign of bolting. He managed to grab a rein just in time. The horse snorted and threw his head up a couple of times.

Wakely glanced inside the wagon. There were two trunks underneath the buckboard seat. Excitement seized him like a fever as he stared at it. They must contain the money. He finally turned his attention to the tarpaulin. He wondered whether there was more money underneath it. He pulled it impatiently aside. He found himself staring at a white, frightened face. It was not the face however that riveted his attention, but the revolver in the youngster's hand. At that moment Gill fired at point-blank range.

16

Back at the staging post between Stoneville and Herford the deputy sheriff, Dave Phillips, was slowly recovering from his wound. He had been tended night and day by Harriet and her constant nursing had helped his recovery. His fever had gone and the wound in his shoulder was less painful than it had been. He was so far along the road to recovery that he even felt that he could get up.

'Are you sure you are well enough?' asked a worried Harriet.

'Of course I am. I'll put my arm in a sling so that I won't damage my shoulder. Then I'll just go for a little stroll.'

'I'll come with you to make sure you don't go too far.'

'You've been too good to me as it is. I don't want to put you to any more trouble.'

Stagecoach to Damnation

'It's been no trouble,' she said.

With the help of Mrs Cooper she fixed a sling for Dave's arm. 'It's nice to see you're recovering,' stated the old lady, when the bandage was completed.

They set out to walk around the staging post. I wonder how long it will be before I can ride a horse again?' Dave said, gazing wistfully at the horses in the corral.

'By Christmas, I expect,' said Harriet.

'What?' exclaimed Dave. Then, suddenly realizing that she was kidding, he added, 'Very funny.'

She glanced at him and, observing how pale he looked, said, 'You're not going any further.'

'All right,' he conceded. He tried not to show how tired the little jaunt had made him. 'Let's sit down on the seat by the trough.'

They sat down. 'I don't know how to start to try to thank you for taking care of me these past few days,' he began.

'Then don't try,' she said.

'If it wasn't for you I don't know what would have happened to me,' he continued.

'If you don't keep quiet about thanking me I'll hit you on your bad shoulder.' Her smile took any sting out of the words.

He smiled back. They really seemed to get along very well together, he concluded. A feller could do far worse than have Harriet for a wife.

Stagecoach to Damnation

How old was she? Eighteen? She seemed older than that. Probably because of the way her wastrel of a father had dragged her from one town to another during the past couple of years.

Without meaning to he said, 'Can I kiss you?'

'Wh-at?' A startled Harriet was taken completely by surprise.

'I'm sorry – I shouldn't have asked.' He turned away, embarrassed.

To his surprise she answered: 'You can if you like.'

He hadn't kissed many girls – except at Christmas parties and Thanksgiving Day, and weddings and things like that. He had never had a regular girlfriend, possibly because he didn't consider himself the sort of person a girl would want to go out with. He knew he wasn't handsome. Even his mother used to tell him that. 'You're the runt in the litter. But your heart is in the right place. One day you'll make some girl a good husband.'

Harriet was staring in front waiting for him to kiss her. Suddenly he realized he couldn't do it.

'What's the matter?' she asked, as she turned to face him.

'I'm on the wrong side,' he said, 'I can't put my arm around you.'

She burst out laughing. Her laugh was infectious. Suddenly he found himself laughing too.

Stagecoach to Damnation

They were laughing so much it brought Mrs Cooper out of the house.

'It must have been a good joke,' she observed.

'It was,' said Harriet, wiping the tears from her eyes.

'I've just made some coffee,' said the old lady. 'Would you like some?'

Harriet said they would. Dave regretfully concluded that he would have to put his kiss away for another day.

17

He had missed! The realization hit him like a sledge-hammer. His hand had shaken so much at the sight of the terrible face a couple of feet away from him that he had given an involuntary jerk.

He knew as soon as he had fired that the bullet had passed harmlessly above the killer's head. He wasn't used to handling a gun but he knew that he had to get another bullet off as quickly as possible. However he found his hand was held in a vice-like grip which prevented any further movement. He whimpered as he tried to tear his hand free.

Wakely began to prise his fingers away from the gun. Gill could smell his foul breath as his head came closer to him. Wakely was far stronger than Gill, and although the young man tried to hang on to his revolver like a limpet Wakely was obviously succeeding in his efforts. He punctuated his struggle with grunts and with both hands now firmly on the revolver it would only be a short while before he would succeed.

Gill's whimpering had now changed to sobbing as he realized that his expectation of a long life was rapidly decreasing. He tried to roll away from Wakely's menacing presence. The movement brought an unexpected bonus, since the horses, who had already been on tenterhooks after the gunshots, became more frightened by the unexpected activity in the wagon. They began to move forward. Wakely was forced to jump aside to avoid the wheel running over his foot. This gave Gill a brief respite from the excruciating pain of having his fingers prised away from the revolver.

The horses, sensing that they were entering a new and desirable phase in their lives which excluded being tugged at by someone at the end of reins, began to move forward more quickly, leaving Wakely behind. At first he made a run to try to catch them up, but their taste for freedom exceeded his burst of speed and they were soon galloping along. When Wakely had approached the wagon he had carelessly dropped his Winchester on the ground in order to leave his hands free to examine the money. Now he dashed back, picked up the gun and began to fire rapidly at the fast-moving wagon. However the combination of the wagon's disappearing into the distance

Stagecoach to Damnation

in a cloud of dust and his aim being less than accurate due to the frustration he was experiencing at seeing all that lovely money disappearing upset his aim and none of his bullets found any worthwhile target. He chose the only alternative course of action available to him – he jumped on his horse and began to race after the runaway wagon.

Unlike the horses, who were revelling in their new-found freedom and would be happy if it would go on for ever, Gill quickly realized that the state of affairs couldn't last. His quick glance to the rear confirmed the fact that Wakely was on their tail, and that realistically one horse following a wagon would be bound to catch the vehicle up after a certain distance. The only slight thing in his favour at the moment was that the horses didn't seem to want any guiding. They were quite happily following the trail as though they had spent much of their lives on it.

Wakely was gaining. There was no doubt about that. Perhaps he should try a few shots with his revolver. There were two factors against that. In the first place he didn't have a snowball's chance of hitting Wakely, travelling along as he was in a bouncing, swaying wagon. In the second place his fingers, due to Wakely's recent attention, felt as though they had been trodden on by an elephant.

He glanced behind again. Wakely was now only

Stagecoach to Damnation

a hundred or so yards away. Soon he would catch up with him and then it would be goodbye Gill. Wait a minute! An exciting thought hit him. In his books he had read how Alexander, the Greek general, had made his escape from his pursuers after ransacking a town by throwing all the valuables his men had taken – gold, diamonds, ornaments and so on – away as they galloped off. The Persian general following them had urged his men to ignore the fortune which was scattered on the trail and go after the Greeks and kill them. The greed of the Persian soldiers was too great and they ignored their general and set about collecting the scattered treasure. So Alexander and his men escaped.

Gill saw it as his last chance. He picked up one of the chests and began emptying it along the trail as the horses galloped along. Dollar bills of various denominations began to float idly to the ground. Some, caught in a stray zephyr sailed daintily upwards into the air before joining their companions on the trail.

Wakely reined in his horse and stared in disbelief at the money which was lying around him. Much of it had stayed in the chest which had burst open and fallen on its side. A large number of bills which had fallen out had formed a neat pile nearby, like drifting snow after a heavy fall. Gill, who had at last grabbed the reins slowed the horses down and stared back at Wakely. He was near enough to see the expression on his face. To Gill's surprise Wakely's face had broken into a smile. Gill could see that he was even laughing.

Gill's reaction was one of relief. It was obvious that Wakely was going to ignore him and collect the money. There was one other surprise for Gill in Wakely's reaction. After his laughter Wakely took his rifle in his hands. For one frightening moment Gill thought that Wakely was going to shoot at him. Instead he pointed his rifle in the air and fired it. It was Wakely's way of saying 'thank you'.

Gill too aimed his revolver in the air and fired it. If translated into vocal terms it would have been 'you're welcome'.

18

Later that afternoon there was another meeting in the sheriff's office. The two bodies had been collected by Gill who had driven the wagon once more to the spot where Wakely had ambushed them. He had taken two men with him whom the sheriff had sworn in as deputies. Gill had known there would be no hope of finding Wakely – he would have disappeared over the horizon hours ago. Still it was nice to have the reassuring physical presence of two armed men.

They had found the corpses without any difficulty and loaded them on to the the wagon. Gill and his two companions had then searched for any banknotes that Wakely might have left behind, but the vicinity had been picked as clean as if by vultures.

Now the inquest on the day's events was being held. Gill had gone over his part in the events again – this time for the benefit of McCloud, the bank-manager. Whereas the sheriff had earlier congratulated Gill on getting out alive from a perilous situation, McCloud was more concerned about the money.

'Was there any need to toss a whole chest out for the robber?' demanded McCloud.

'I didn't have much choice,' retorted Gill sharply. 'It was either that or he'd have killed me.'

'You could just have tipped some of the money out,' persisted McCloud. 'He might have been satisfied with that.'

'How was I supposed to know how much he would be satisfied with?' Gill was on his feet and shouting by now. 'Was I supposed to ask him, Mr Gunman, will twenty thousand dollars be enough?'

McCloud, who had the reddish face of many of those with sandy hair, went even redder. 'There's no need to adopt that tone with me young man,' he blustered.

The sheriff sat impassively surveying the scene. Up to now he had always regarded his deputy as a bit of a greenhorn, but now he was showing another side to his character which secretly pleased him.

'Are you going to sit there and let one of your staff insult me like this?' stormed McCloud.

'If you are more concerned about your precious

Stagecoach to Damnation

money than my deputy's life then the answer is yes,' said the sheriff.

McCloud realized that he had gone too far with his outburst. 'I'm sorry,' he said. Although it hurt his ulcer to say the words he forced himself to address Gill. 'Please accept my apology.'

'I accept it,' replied Gill.

'Right, that's cleared the air,' said the sheriff in businesslike tones. 'Let's discuss what we have to do next.'

'We've got to catch the robber,' said McCloud positively.

'I agree,' said the sheriff. 'I've got an artist coming in shortly. He'll draw a picture of the robber as Gill describes him. We'll post it up all over town. Somebody must know him.'

'Yes, that's a good idea,' said McCloud. 'But what if he's already taken to the trail?'

'I'll be getting a posse together. The earliest we'll be able to start will be first thing in the morning. I'll have an Indian tracker with us. Hopefully we might be able to pick up his trail.'

'Yes, that might help,' concurred McCloud.

'What about the bank?' demanded the sheriff. 'Are you going to close it?'

'No, we'll keep it open as usual. After all, the money that was due to go to Damnation wasn't a part of our assets.'

'What about Damnation?' asked Gill. 'Will the

Stagecoach to Damnation

delivery of the rest of the money go ahead?'

'I don't see why not,' said McCloud. 'There was a further fifty thousand in the other chest. It will be enough to start a small bank in Damnation. Later we can send more money and gold to them.'

'You're not going to send another wagon, are you?' asked the sheriff, with some dismay, knowing that he would have to provide safety for the wagon.

'No.' McCloud leaned forward confidentially. 'Between these four walls, I'm going to send it by stagecoach. Though the people on the stage won't know about it, of course.'

19

When Cam heard about the posse he volunteered to join it. 'It's better than hanging about here for the next few days,' he told Doris.

'And I thought you'd be quite happy keeping me company,' she pouted.

'Nothing would please me more, but duty calls,' he said, with an impassive face.

'Huh, some duty,' she said, scornfully. 'It's just an excuse to go off riding for a couple of days.'

'Never mind, we'll soon be on our way to Damnation,' he informed her.

To his surprise she said, 'Take care,' and kissed him lightly on the cheek.

The posse gathered in the town square. There were about two dozen riders. Among those who joined it was Ed Smith. He could afford to take time off from distilling his whiskey since there was very little he could do at the moment.

Stagecoach to Damnation

The sheriff began to address them. 'This is the man we're searching for.' He held up a sheet of paper with a face on it, 'We don't know his name but he's very dangerous. He's killed two men and almost killed a third.' He began to pass some copies of the artist's impression of Wakely's face around. 'He's got a scar across his face,' he continued. 'This is the one feature you will be able to recognize him by.'

When they had all examined the drawing the sheriff called out. 'Right. Let's go.'

They trooped off to a muted cheer from the small crowd who had gathered to watch them go. Two of the onlookers had particular interests in the riders. Doris was one of them. She watched Cam as he rode off. Her heart gave a slight lurch and she gave him a brief wave as he disappeared around the corner, although he hadn't noticed her presence.

What was she doing standing like a schoolgirl and waving Cam off? He was nothing to her, and she meant nothing to him. She had sworn after her last love-affair that she had finished with men. In fact she had sworn the same thing after her last three love-affairs. But after she had finished with Steve, barely two months previously, she had irrevocably and positively decided she had finished with men. That was the main reason why she had decided to go to one of the most God-forsaken towns she had ever heard of — Damnation. She had decided to bury herself in her work. She would spend a few years setting up a business. Then, as a successful businesswoman and still only just over thirty years of age, she would start looking around for a suitable husband. Instead of which Cam had come on the scene. Damn him! And damn all men!

The other traveller on the stage who was standing on the fringe of the crowd keeping out of sight was a man with a nondescript face who would never stand out in a crowd anyhow. He was Sterne.

Questions were buzzing round in his head like angry bees. Why had Wakely decided to go on his own and hold up the bank's delivery of money to Damnation? Why had he ignored his plan to hire two other men and hold up the wagon? He had seen the artist's picture of Wakely and he had to admit it was a good likeness, except for the scar down the side of his face. Wakely hadn't been sporting a scar the last time he had seen him. The only explanation he could come up with was that Wakely had been responsible for the fire that had killed Melton and that somehow he had received a blow which had scarred his face. Sterne looked at the artist's picture again. Wakely had always been an ugly bastard, but now with the scar down the side of his face he

Stagecoach to Damnation

looked positively frightening. Well there was nothing he could do except go back to the hotel and wait and see what would happen. There was nothing to connect him with Wakely. He really had nothing to fear. He would just be an innocent bystander to events. All he hoped was that Wakely would get shot by one of the posse. It would serve him right for not falling in with his carefully laid plan. He for one would certainly not give a damn if the posse brought Wakely's corpse back with them.

20

The posse didn't find Wakely. They returned two days later, dusty and dishevelled. Gill went straight to the sheriff's office.

'There was no sign of him,' he explained. 'The Indian picked up his trail. It was leading to Damnation. It's pretty obvious that he was heading there. He's probably gone on past the town now and gone over the border into Canada.'

'I never thought you'd find him,' said the sheriff. 'But I had to go along with the act to pacify McCloud.'

'Yes, I suppose so,' said Gill, who, although the search had been unsuccessful, had enjoyed the experience of riding with the posse. One of the main reasons for this was that the others in the group had regarded him as a bit of a hero. After all, he had struggled face to face with the man who had already killed two men. And he had survived to tell the tale. Many of the riders had previously regarded him as a rather ineffective deputy who had accepted the post because nobody else had applied for it. But now they had obviously changed their minds. They had offered him a variety of gifts from cigars to chewing-tobacco to show their new-found respect for him.

'While you've been away, I've found out one thing,' said the sheriff. 'The man you've been searching for is named Wakely. One of the hotel-keepers in town recognized him. He stayed in the Cock and Bull for a couple of nights although he didn't have the scar at that time. Maybe it would be worth your having another talk with the owner. He's a man named Sheffield.'

'Right,' said Gill.

Cam had mostly kept himself to himself while he was on the trail with the posse. He was content to go along for the ride. The only person he had any long conversation with was Ed Smith, who happened to draw alongside him on the second day.

Ed introduced himself. 'I'm the town whiskey supplier,' stated Ed.

'I've never met a whiskey supplier before,' said Cam. 'I've met a lot of people though who've drunk it.'

'Well, I came into it by accident,' said Ed. He explained how he would have been forced to leave

Stagecoach to Damnation

Herford if he had continued to make his patent medicine. And so he had changed to making whiskey instead. 'I just brought a large still back from Stoneville,' he added.

'I remember you now,' said Cam. 'I was with the stage when we met you on the way to Stoneville.'

'That's right,' said Ed. 'A few miles further on we came across a deputy sheriff who had been shot by an Indian. We took him on to the staging post. My daughter has nursed him and now he's well on his way to recovering.'

'I wonder what happened to the Indian?' said Cam.

'I can tell you. We came across his body not far away from the spot where we found the deputy. The lawman had put half a dozen bullets into him.'

A short while later Ed again rode alongside Cam. 'I don't suppose you'd like to sample my whiskey when we get back to Herford.'

'Why not? I've sampled many different whiskeys in my time. I'm always ready to try another one.'

'I'll be opening a bottle. I've got to try it out to make sure that it's all right. I don't want to drink on my own. So maybe you'd care to join me.'

'As soon as we get back I'll have a bath and join you.'

Ed gave him directions how to find his wagon.

They rode into Herford an hour or so later. It was obvious to the bystanders that their venture had been in vain. Cam rode up to the hotel. Doris watched him with relief that he had returned safely. At least she would have some refreshing company at dinner that evening. She would have a long hot bath and take her time going down to dinner. Who knows, perhaps they would go for a stroll after dinner.

When she finally appeared at the dining-room she was surprised that only the reverend and his wife were at the table. 'I thought I heard Mr Grayling returning.' She ventured the comment knowing that Mrs Beeson was regarding her knowingly.

'He's come and gone,' said the preacher's wife, with obvious satisfaction at getting one over on the fellow-traveller who wore the low-cut dress. Doris tried to conceal her disappointment by taking an inordinate time to unfurl her napkin.

Meanwhile Cam was sampling Ed's whiskey. 'It's very good,' he announced at last.

'You don't think it could do with more maturing?' Ed fussed over it like a young mother with a baby.

'Maybe a little,' agreed Cam, trying another dram.

'I can make fifty bottles with this new still,' explained Ed.

Stagecoach to Damnation

'You'll have no difficulty selling this,' announced Cam, as he accepted another drink.

Half an hour later he had lost count of the number of drams he had drunk. Both men had become maudlin.

'I miss my daughter, Harriet,' said Ed.

'I miss Doris,' said Cam.

'Who's Doris?' demanded Ed.

'She's on the stage with me. You should see her. She's got a figure like . . .' He waved his hands to show how curvaceous Doris's figure was.

'I want to buy Harriet a new dress,' said Ed. 'I'll be able to afford it with all the money I'll be getting from my whiskey. Have another one,' he added.

'No thanks,' said Cam getting up unsteadily. 'I have to ride shotgun in the morning.'

'I don't think you know one end of a gun from the other,' said Ed.

For some unaccountable reason Cam thought the remark was one of the funniest he had ever heard. He began to laugh. Ed joined him. Soon they were laughing and holding each other up at the same time.

'I must go now,' said Cam, finally.

'Happy journey,' said Ed.

Cam succeeded in making his way back to the hotel. It was obvious from the pervading darkness that everybody had gone to bed. Cam crept

Stagecoach to Damnation

as quietly up the stairs as he could – only succeeding in stumbling on two occasions. Doris heard him pass her room. Where did I ever get the idea from that I was attracted to a drunk like that, she thought icily.

21

The following morning the stage started off early. Cam was nursing the worst head he had ever had and was only dimly aware of the activity that was going on around him.

'Bad head?' asked Doris, witheringly, as she got into the stage.

'It'll get better,' Cam informed her.

Lawson had loaded the chest from the bank while the travellers were having breakfast. McCloud had informed him that there would be a bonus for him if he managed to deliver the chest safely to the bank in Damnation. Lawson decided that it didn't take a genius to work out that the chest contained a good sum of money.

'Hooah!' he yelled, and with a crack of the whip the stage began to roll.

The horses began to slowly eat up the miles to the staging post. In all there were three posts between Herford and Damnation. The passengers settled down to their usual routine of either trying to sleep or staring out through the window at the view. Without realizing it they passed the spot where Wakely had held up the bank's wagon a few days before. In fact the only person who would have recognized the place would have been Cam, since that was where the posse started from when it had began its search for the robber. However Cam was not taking too much notice of where exactly the stage was in relation to its journey due to the fact that his head felt as though it was twice its normal size and there was a little man inside trying to drill his way out.

He swore he would never touch Ed's whiskey again. In fact he would never touch any whiskey again. Not even a single glass.

While most of the passengers inside the stage were in a languorous state induced by its monotonous movement, the mind of one man was brimming with excitement. Sterne could hardly keep himself from fidgeting at the exciting knowledge he possessed. However, he knew that any excessive movements would be observed by the others who might start wondering what ailed the usually quiet, unobtrusive man.

Sterne knew that the bank had loaded a chest of money on to the stage early that morning! He had spent most of his life watching and waiting.

Stagecoach to Damnation

He had always kept his ear close to the ground. That was why he was a successful robber. This morning his vigilance had paid off. He had got up early as usual. He had gone outside to see if anything unusual had been going on. And his reward was to see the chest being transferred from the bank's wagon to the stage. He had kept out of sight round a corner, but he was able to peer round and view the transaction. It was all over in a few minutes. But he knew that what he had seen would make him a rich man.

There must have been two chests on the wagon that Wakely had held up. Yes, that made sense since you wouldn't expect the whole amount of one hundred thousand dollars to be bundled into one chest. So Wakely had had one. And here was the other, only a couple of feet away, tucked under the buckboard, covered with a tarpaulin. He wished he could express his excitement in some way – such as whistling. But wisely he kept quiet.

While Sterne was trying to conceal his delight, Doris was just as busily hiding her disappointment. The last thing she wanted was that old cow sitting opposite her to realize that she had been attracted to Cam, and that, because of his behaviour last night, everything had instantly changed. She had been led astray by her heart before, but one type of man she could never consider as a lover was a drunkard. Maybe it was because her father had been a drunkard. She could vividly picture the nights when he had come home drunk and there had been quarrels and fights and in some cases it had ended with the china being smashed, and on more than one occasion even the furniture. She could never understand how her mother had suffered such humiliating treatment for so long. Although, to be fair, in the end they had left him in one of his drunken stupors and caught a stage and gone to live with her aunt in Cotterton. She had never seen her father again. And if Cam was a drunkard, and all the evidence pointed that way, once this journey was over, she would never want to see him again either.

Sterne, having savoured the initial joy of the discovery of the money, realized that he was now left with a big problem. How was he going to steal the money? Also, when was he going to steal it?

It was obvious that he had to steal it before the stage reached Damnation, since once the money was in the bank there was very little chance of him getting his hands on it. So it would have to be before the stage reached Damnation. That gave him three days. In that time he had to devise a plan and put it into action.

The snag was there was no way he could do it on his own. He had to have an accomplice. He knew the passengers on the stage by now, having spent almost a week in their company. The only person who remotely fitted the bill was the gambler, Melrose.

There was one advantage in approaching Melrose – he was broke. While they had been staying at Herford, Melrose had joined a gambling-school in a less than reputable saloon named the Cock and Bull. Acting on his habitual assumption that it paid to know as much about his travelling companions as possible, he had followed Melrose into the saloon. It was soon obvious that although Melrose was a reasonably proficient gambler he was not in the same league as a couple of the professionals he was playing with. The result was, although he had managed to hold his own on the first night, the story had changed on the second night. Melrose had lost all his money, even the silver watch which he had carried in his waistcoat pocket. So the young man was a perfect target for his aim of getting an accomplice to help him with the robbery. He could hardly conceal his impatience at the stage's slow progress. He could hardly wait until that evening when they would reach the first staging post and he could approach Melrose.

22

Wakely, whom the Sheriff of Herford had assumed was already safe in Damnation, was in fact barely half-way there. In fact if the posse had continued its progress for another couple of miles instead of turning back they would have discovered him. The reason for his lack of rapid progress was that his horse was lame. It had suddenly stumbled and had almost thrown him. He jumped off and examined the horse's foot, thinking that the trouble was probably a loose shoe. However it was obvious that the animal had pulled a muscle. Which had left Wakely cursing his bad luck.

His only chance now of reaching Damnation was to get hold of another horse. He had passed the first staging post a few miles back. He knew there were spare horses there. He reasoned that his best chance was to retrace his steps and steal one of their horses. In view of the fact that darkness would soon descend he wouldn't be able to do anything about it until the next day. He took the saddle off the horse, tied the animal to a convenient tree and prepared to spend another night on the mountain slope.

Things weren't working out, either, for his one-time companion in crime, Sterne, who had assumed that at the end of their journey for the day it would be a simple matter to have a meeting with Melrose where they could discuss his plan to rob the stage. Unfortunately, when the day's journey was over, and they had sat down for their evening meal as usual, Melrose had suddenly excused himself complaining of a bad stomach. He had gone up to his room with the stage post owner, a man named Yardley, following him. The other travellers had waited anxiously for his return. When Yardley finally reappeared he informed them that Melrose was not seriously ill, but probably needed a good night's rest. After the delay in Herford the travellers breathed a collective sigh of relief. Yardley added that apparently Melrose had been having these stomach pains for a few days and while they were staying in Herford Melrose bought some patent medicine from a man named Ed Smith. Possibly the medicine hadn't helped Melrose's condition. In fact it had probably done him more harm than good. On

Stagecoach to Damnation

hearing the verdict Cam pulled his hat down over his face. Doris caught the movement out of the corner of her eye.

While Cam was enjoying his last cigar out on the veranda before turning in, Doris came out to join him. She had sworn that she wouldn't speak to him again, but the way he had pulled his hat down over his face as though to disassociate himself with the person named Ed Smith, had intrigued her. Also, she told herself, the journey was so boring that if she didn't speak to somebody soon she would go mad.

'What was all that about?' she asked, as she leaned on the rail by his side.

'I don't know what you mean,' he said, pretending innocence.

'Oh, come on, don't play games with me. You know this Ed Smith, don't you?'

'Yes,' he confessed.

'You didn't take any of his medicine did you?' There was a trace of alarm in her voice at the realization that perhaps last night he had been ill after all and not drunk.

'Yes and no.'

'What do you mean, yes and no?'

'I did take something he had concocted, but I'd hardly describe it as medicine.'

'Moonshine,' she exclaimed with sudden enlightenment. 'You had been drinking moonshine.'

Stagecoach to Damnation

'He's making whiskey which he'll be selling to the public,' explained Cam patiently.

'And you were his unofficial tester, I suppose,' she said, icily.

'Yes. In my opinion I don't think it was quite ready,' he informed her.

She turned to walk away. 'That's no excuse for you ending up the way you were last night,' she said, coldly.

He grabbed her arm forcing her to stop in her tracks. 'What's this with you and drink?' he demanded.

'My father was a drunkard,' she snapped.

'I'm not a drunk,' he stated calmly. 'I often go for weeks without a drink. Last night was a one-off occasion. You can believe me or not.'

For a few moments neither moved as they stared at each other in the dim light. Finally she whispered, 'I believe you.'

After that it seemed only natural that she should end up in his arms.

23

Sterne was forced to wait until they reached the next staging post before tackling Melrose about helping him to steal the money. However he had gleaned one piece of knowledge the previous night, namely that Lawson took the chest to his room with him. This would give him an ideal opportunity to go to Lawson's room, knock on the door under some pretext or other, then, when Lawson opened it, he would club him and take the money. Melrose would be waiting with the horses at the ready. It would only be a matter of jumping on them and galloping off into the night.

All the passengers regarded Melrose solicitously when they came down for breakfast, but none with more interest than Sterne. He was relieved that, in answer to their questions Melrose confessed that he felt a lot better. By contrast Mrs Beeson regarded Doris with interest. To her Doris looked like the cat that had got the cream. She declared as much to her husband later in their room when they were getting ready to leave. He agreed with her without actually knowing what she was talking about.

They set off for the next staging post, Sterne knowing that this would be his last chance to steal the money.

While the stage was travelling at its usual slow pace towards the staging post, Wakely was travelling even more slowly. During the night his horse had been making pitiful whining noises. Wakely had examined him by the light of the moon. He was lying on his side and sweating profusely. It was obvious to Wakely that there was something seriously wrong with him. He'd see how the horse was in the morning but he had little hope that he'd be able to ride him again.

Dawn confirmed what the night had indicated. The horse was too ill to stand up. Wakely put his revolver to its head and pulled the trigger. The sound of the shot seemed to echo for ages before finally dying away. Wakely collected his waterbottle, his rifle and the saddle-bag containing his money and set off to walk to the staging post.

For once, to Doris, the journey did not seem too long. Her thoughts dwelt on the night before. Their love-making in the barn had been torrid and unrestrained. It had confirmed that Cam was the sort of man she would willingly spend a great deal of time with. A whole lifetime in fact. She looked up and caught Mrs Beeson studying her. For one delicious moment she felt like winking at her. She pictured the old cow's reaction if she did. She couldn't refrain from smiling as she closed her eyes against the low morning sun.

Up on the buckboard Cam was also thinking about last night. A man could do worse than settle down with a handsome woman like Doris. She was great in the sack as well as being excellent company. What more could a man ask? Anyhow it was about time he stopped chopping and changing from one job to another. He was over thirty and once one passed that age it was settling-down time. He'd saved some money and he'd have a nice fat bonus after the successful completion of this trip. Yes, maybe it was time for him to settle down.

They reached the staging post without mishap. Tomorrow they would be on the final leg of their journey to Damnation. The thought that they were nearing their destination gave everyone a feeling of *bonhomie*. Doris noticed that even Mrs Beeson looked more relaxed after dinner. To add to the atmosphere the man who kept the staging post, a bald-headed man named Kennedy, began to play an old piano which stood in the corner of the room. After a couple of tunes he asked if anyone would give a song.

'What about you?' Doris mischievously asked Cam.

'If I sang all the horses in the corral would bolt,' he answered. 'What about you?' he countered.

She sighed. 'All right. If you insist,' She crossed to the piano and whispered something in the pianist's ear. After he had found the right chord, she began to sing, *The Last Rose of Summer*.

To Cam's surprise Doris had a lovely voice. It soared up to the high notes without any effort. She held her notes like a professional singer and kept in perfect time. She held everyone spellbound as they listened to the familiar words. The haunting refrain seemed to echo around the old room, hinting of the past when other singers held the stage.

Doris finished to a burst of applause which went on and on. To her surprise Mrs Beeson came up to her.

'That was lovely, my dear,' she said and Doris noticed that there were tears in her eyes.

Her husband, too, stepped forward. 'If you intend staying in Damnation,' he stated, 'I'll be forming a choir. I would consider it an honour to hear your beautiful voice in our church.'

'I'll think about it,' Doris promised. She crossed over to Cam.

'I don't know what to say,' he said, for once at a loss for words.

'Don't say anything,' she said, kissing him on the lips.

At that moment the door burst open. A man stood there with a rifle in one hand and a revolver in the other. 'Don't anyone move,' he snarled.

It was Wakely.

24

They all stood staring in mute shock at the sudden apparition in the doorway. The only exception was Sterne, who greeted Wakely like a long lost brother.

'Wakely!' he cried, stepping forward.

Wakely took the unexpected meeting in his stride. 'Keep them covered,' he commanded.

Sterne obeyed. 'All of you in the corner,' he said, waving a threatening revolver.

They obeyed, Cam being more reluctant than the rest. So the horrible thing in the doorway was Wakely, the robber they had been following. How had he suddenly turned up here? Wakely was now consulting with Sterne in a whisper. Cam, who had automatically put a protective arm around Doris, wished he could hear the conversation.

Suddenly Wakely disappeared through the

Stagecoach to Damnation

doorway. If anyone had assumed that it gave them a chance to escape the hope was quickly dispelled by Sterne, who put a bullet into the floor near enough to make them jump back.

'You'll all stay here until I say so,' said Sterne.

The preacher had put his hands together and was praying silently.

'What are you doing?' demanded Sterne.

'Praying for your salvation,' the reverend answered.

'You'll want to pray for your own,' said Sterne with a smirk as he waved the gun threateningly. 'Particularly after Wakely has finished with you.'

Cam noticed for the umpteenth time how putting a gun in a man's hand changes his personality completely. Sterne, who up to now had been a self-effacing, nondescript person, had suddenly become a puffed-out peacock of a man as he strutted importantly in front of them. If he, Cam, had been on his own he would have tried to have taken him, even though the odds were stacked against him. But with the women present and the other passengers there was nothing he could do but wait and see what would happen.

Wakely returned. 'I've picked a horse,' he told Sterne.

Cam noticed that he was not carrying the saddle-bag he'd had over his shoulder when he had arrived ten minutes earlier. He was still carrying the two guns though. Sterne pointed his gun at Lawson. 'We'll go up to your room and get the chest with the rest of the money in it,' he announced.

For some reason Lawson hesitated. Was it because he still harboured some sort of loyalty to the bank for entrusting him with the money? Whatever thoughts were spinning through his head as he hesitated they were interrupted by Wakely's next remark.

'My friend told you to move. I don't like people who don't obey our orders.' So saying he shot Lawson in the head and a mixture of Lawson's blood, bones and brains splattered on the floor as he fell.

Gasps of horror rose from the remaining travellers. Doris buried her head in Cam's shoulder.

'You,' said Wakely, pointing to Melrose, 'go with him to carry the chest.' Melrose obeyed with such alacrity that in normal circumstances it would have been amusing. But these were far from normal circumstances, Cam concluded, when you were dealing with a madman like Wakely.

Sterne returned with Melrose, who was carrying the chest.

'You,' Wakely addressed Kennedy. 'Get me a saddle-bag.'

The old man disappeared through a door at the back. Sterne placed the chest on the floor. It was locked.

Stagecoach to Damnation

'I suppose he's got the key,' said Wakely, indicating the bloodied mess of a head on the floor.

'Do you want me to get it?' demanded Melrose, eagerly.

'It doesn't matter,' said Wakely, shooting the lock off.

They watched as he tipped the money out and began to put it into the saddle-bag. None of them had seen so much money before with the exception of the banker, Bridges, and they stared with interest as the saddle-bag began to fill. Finally the robber had almost emptied the chest. He glanced around at the watchers.

'You'll never see as much money as this again,' he informed them.

His gaze rested on Doris. He was down to the last few notes, but instead of putting them in the saddle-bag he stepped up to her. Suddenly he seized her. Sterne's gun moved warningly at Cam's involuntary movement.

The others watched in horror as Wakely began to kiss Doris while with his free hand he pushed the handful of dollar bills down inside her dress. This time Cam could not contain himself. He stepped forward and hit Wakely full on the chin.

Cam was a big man who might have done well in the boxing-ring, as the result of his blow testified. Wakely went down without a sound. Cam was not able to exult in his achievement because the next moment Sterne hit him on the head with the butt of his Colt. And darkness descended.

25

When Cam recovered he found that his head was in Doris's lap. He was conscious that he had a splitting headache. He also realized that Doris was weeping.

'It's all right. I've recovered already,' he said, sitting up and stifling a groan.

'I'm not crying about you,' she said, kissing him briefly. 'I knew you'd come round. I'm crying because of my stock.'

He thought he hadn't heard her correctly. 'What stock?' he asked.

'There.' She pointed to the window through which a red glare could be seen.

It took Cam a few seconds to realize that he was witnessing a fire. It was burning merrily outside. 'It's the stage,' he said with disbelief in his tones.

His observation brought a renewed burst of

Stagecoach to Damnation

crying from Doris. Mrs Beeson took her in her arms to comfort her. Cam staggered to his feet.

'That devil Wakely set fire to the stage,' said the minister.

'He also shot all the horses,' said the banker.

'Have you got any more horses in the back corral?' Cam asked Kennedy.

'Sure, I've got three I always keep there.'

'I'll take one,' said Cam. 'I'll fix up to pay you for him when I come back.'

Doris had instantly forgotten her own troubles and rushed to Cam's side. 'You're not going anywhere,' she cried. 'Don't let him go.' She addressed the assembled company. 'He'll get killed.'

'I don't think it'll be a wise move,' said the banker. 'You've just had a bump on the head. And anyhow there are two of them against you. Two killers,' he added.

'Never mind about the stock,' she pleaded. 'It's only material. We'll build it up again. Please don't go. I'm begging you.' So saying she went down on her knees and seized his hand.

'I've got to go,' he said. 'If I don't go I'll never forgive myself.'

'Let him go,' said the reverend, quietly.

'No, no, you can't,' sobbed Doris, holding on to him with both hands.

Cam gently disentangled himself. 'I'll be back,

Stagecoach to Damnation

I promise,' he said. There was such a big lump in his throat as he headed for the door that he couldn't trust himself to say any more.

Outside the cool air hit him. He staggered and would have fallen except for the fact that Kennedy had brought a horse round for him and he was able to hang on to the saddle.

'Are you all right?' asked Kennedy, with some concern.

'Just show me which direction they went in,' answered Cam.

'Well that's the funny thing,' said the other. 'I'd have expected them to go north – to the Canadian border. Instead they went south. They had a short argument about it, but finally the one with the scar on his face—'

'Wakely,' supplied Cam.

'He won the argument. He said he wasn't going to any foreign country.'

'So they're heading for Herford,' said Cam thoughtfully.

'That's right.'

'Thanks for the help,' said Cam, preparing to leave.

'There's one other thing,' said Kennedy. 'You'll need these.' He handed Cam a gunbelt with two revolvers in it. 'These were last used to scare away some Indians. but I've always kept them greased. I knew that one day they'd come in handy.'

Stagecoach to Damnation

Cam accepted the guns. He rode slowly away, passing the stage which was now a grotesque outline of its former self with tiny fires burning along the frame. Cam was tempted to look back at the window of the staging post where he knew the others would be watching. Particularly one person. Doris. He knew though that if he looked back it would lower his desire to go ahead with his self-appointed task. One more sight of Doris's tearful face through the window could weaken his resolve so much that he might turn back. And he knew that he could never live with himself if he did.

26

As Cam rode along he found that the combination of the pleasant movement of the horse and the cool night air on his brow helped to dispel his headache. He tried to calculate how far the robbers were ahead of him – two miles, three miles, five miles? He finally gave it up as a futile exercise. The important thing to do was to get to Herford as quickly as he could. Perhaps once he got there he could inform the sheriff who could get a posse together to hunt down Wakely and Sterne. He'd probably join the posse himself. In which case it would be ironic that he would be in a posse trying to catch Wakely a few days after he had been a member of the first one.

He hoped they would be able to hunt down Wakely. He had never come across anyone who treated human life so cheaply. There had been a rumour when he was in the posse that Wakely had killed the young man who had been working in the bank and also his mother. And had then set fire to their house. He hadn't believed it, thinking that no human being could be responsible for such a deed. But now, having seen Wakely, he was prepared to believe anything about him.

Cam glanced up at the moon. He knew that a great deal depended on that round yellow orb up there. If it stayed away from any clouds and continued to light the way for the rest of the night, then they should all be well on their way to Herford by sun-up. It was a full moon. What they used to call back home in Wyoming a lover's moon. Well, he had found someone to love, there was no doubt about that. And somebody who loved him. He pictured Doris as she clung to him pleading with him not to leave. He knew that the only thing he wanted to do in the whole world was to catch up with the two robbers ahead of him and then return safely to his lovely Doris.

In fact the moon did stay out for the night. Cam made good time. They passed the place where the posse had started from earlier in the week. Cam knew that they were now only a few miles from Herford. The sky had been lightening for the past half-hour. Everything seemed in favour of him arriving in Herford and notifying the sheriff, who should be able to get a posse together before many of the inhabitants started on their daily round of work. Cam was concentrating on this pleasant scenario when there was the sound of a shot accompanied by a bullet whizzing an inch or so past his head, shattering his illusions. The riders in front had obviously become aware of the fact that he was following them.

There were some trees to the right. Cam quickly swung the horse into their midst as the second shot sounded. The bullet took some of the leaves from a tree close to Cam's head, but otherwise did no damage. Cam rode the horse deeper into the safety of the trees. The horse needed no second bidding.

When he had gone a couple of hundred yards into what Cam realized was a fairly extensive wood, he dismounted. He tied his horse to one of the trees. Drawing his guns he crept cautiously back to where he had ridden off the trail. As he edged along the thought occurred to him that he had been lucky in that they had shot at him when he was near the trees. He supposed he had also been lucky in that daylight hadn't yet arrived, which had made the rifle-shots more difficult to aim than they could have been.

Cam stopped when he was about fifty yards from the trail. He couldn't see very far along the trail but on the other hand he was fairly sure they couldn't spot him either. After another

Stagecoach to Damnation

couple of rifle-shots in his direction, which missed by several feet, he was more than ever convinced that he had found a secure hiding-place. If they came into the wood on foot all he would have to do would be to go further back into its cover. He could have stayed here all night if needs be, playing hide-and-seek with them, and they wouldn't be able to winkle him out. The important thing was not to fire any shots in retaliation to their own. If he did they would realize the general direction where he was hiding and would close in on him.

To his surprise he heard Sterne's voice shouting. 'Cam, we know you're in there. Come on out and we'll make a deal.'

The voice wasn't as far away as Cam had imagined it would be. Probably only about a hundred yards. He kept perfectly still. What was this deal that Sterne was on about?

It was a couple of minutes later when Sterne spoke again. A couple of minutes in which they were probably scanning every tree hoping for any sign of movement. Cam knew there was none.

'Listen, Cam, you could do with some money. You and your girlfriend. She told me on the stage that she wanted to set up a dressmaker's shop in Damnation. Unfortunately her stock has been destroyed. However we can make that up to her. Suppose we give you ten thousand dollars as compensation for her burnt stock. That would be fair, wouldn't it? We give you the money and you ride away from here and stop following us.'

Yes, and a few yards along the trail I'd have a bullet in my back, thought Cam, viciously. He almost hurled the words at them, but just refrained from doing so in time.

Silence reigned. Nothing moved for quite a long time. The sun, which until now had been hiding below the horizon, began to shed a stronger grey light on the scene. Then suddenly Cam could hear them moving around. He could hear them since they made no effort to conceal themselves. They shouted to each other as they went deeper into the wood. Cam assumed it was to try to make sure they did not get too far apart. They shouted 'Hullo', every few seconds. They had passed Cam's hiding place five minutes before and were now so far into the wood that their voices had become muffled.

However the next sound reached Cam clearly. His heart sank as he heard the sound of his horse whinnying in greeting to their calls. In a few seconds he heard the sickening sound of a single shot. He knew his horse would never greet another human being again.

27

About an hour later Cam trudged wearily into Herford. He had confirmed that his horse was indeed dead. After that there was nothing for him to do but to start walking.

It was still early in the morning but there were several people around. Cam knew that the two robbers now had an excellent lead on him and that the chances of his catching them were very slim. By the time the sheriff got a posse together the two would be even further ahead. In fact they could almost have reached Stoneville by the time the posse was ready. Once the robbers were there they could catch a train and they would be free. These depressing thoughts were going through his mind as he was heading for the sheriff's office when he passed a familiar landmark. It was Ed Smith's wagon. He stared at it with renewed interest when he realized that the two horses were harnessed in the shafts.

Cam was staring at the horses when Ed appeared from the shed where he kept his still. 'I'm afraid I'm not open for business,' said Ed automatically. Then, realizing that it was Cam, he added with a welcoming smile, 'Although in your case I'm willing to make an exception.'

'I'm not in the market for whiskey,' said Cam. 'I see that you're ready to move off. Can I ask where you're going?'

'Sure,' said Ed. 'I'm going to fetch my daughter. She's been staying at the staging post between here and Stoneville. She's been there for nearly a week nursing a deputy sheriff. I'm going to fetch her because I need her here. Business is ready to boom and I want her here to help me.'

The staging post, said Cam, to himself. At least it would mean that he would be half-way to Stoneville. Maybe he could borrow a horse and ride into Stoneville and be in time to catch the robbers before they got on a train.

'Can I have a lift with you to the staging post?' asked Cam. 'I'll explain what it's all about on the way.'

'Sure,' said Ed. 'I never refuse a request from one of my drinking buddies.'

Cam jumped up on the buckboard and they set off. On the way Cam recounted the events which had led him to the present position.

'You've certainly had an eventful twenty-four hours,' observed Ed. 'Do you think you've got any chance of catching the robbers?'

'To be honest I think there's only a slim chance,' answered Cam. 'But even a slight chance is worth taking if it means I will catch Wakely.'

Ed glanced at his companion with surprise on hearing the hatred in his voice. He had considered that Cam was a fairly easy-going sort of guy, much like himself in fact. But on hearing the hardness in his voice he hastily revised his opinion.

For the rest of the journey the two lapsed into silence. Cam was busy with his own thoughts and Ed was still suffering for testing his whiskey the previous night.

They reached the staging post at around midday. They had only met a couple of riders on the way and although Ed had stopped and questioned them both had denied seeing two riders on their way to Stoneville, one of whom had a distinctive scar down the side of his face.

Cam assumed that the two robbers had taken what was known as the hilltop road to Stoneville. This road had been used years before by the Indians, who had always felt safer from their enemies travelling along the top of a hill than in the valley. So anyone wishing to attract as little attention as possible would travel by that road.

Stagecoach to Damnation

And the last thing that Wakely and Sterne would want would be to confront too many travellers.

Ed drove the wagon into the staging post. He had called there on a few occasions and Mrs Cooper greeted him as though he were an old friend. 'Your daughter is inside,' she said. 'Perhaps you'd like a cup of coffee before you collect her. What about you?' she asked Cam.

'Coffee would be fine,' said Cam.

While Ed went inside Cam stayed on the front porch. He surveyed the hills which ran parallel with the valley. Wakely and Sterne had passed along that way probably an hour or so ago. His chances of catching them were getting slimmer by the minute, but he'd have to follow his original intention and borrow a horse to take him to Stoneville.

The deputy sheriff came out to meet him. 'Your friend has explained that you are looking for a couple of robbers named Wakely and Sterne,' he said, after introducing himself. 'I know Sterne. I was on my way to arrest him in Herford when I was shot at by an Indian. I've been here ever since recovering from the wound.'

'There's a faint chance I might catch them before they reach Stoneville,' said Cam. 'I'm going to see if I can borrow a horse and get to Stoneville. I'll see the sheriff and explain the position to him.'

Stagecoach to Damnation

'Tell him I'm recovering and I'll be back to work in a few days,' said the deputy with a crooked smile.

In fact Wakely and Sterne were only a few hundred yards away hiding behind a large rock. They had found that the hill road was harder to travel along than they had imagined. The Indians who had ridden that trail were riders who were second to none. They could take the numerous twists and turns and ups and downs at full speed riding bareback. To Wakely and Sterne every unevenness in the terrain meant that their progress had been slowed. Now at last they had reached the staging post. They were hungry and above all thirsty.

First of all they had to watch while the man and the young girl got aboard the wagon. The young girl had kissed the young man who had come out with her from the house for a what seemed to the watchers like an inordinate time. However it was not the young folks they were interested in but the other man, whose coffee had been brought out to him by the old lady.

'It's him,' said Wakely, correctly identifying Cam at that distance.

'He's been a pain in the backside since we had to stop and look for him in the wood,' said Sterne.

'You should have shot him instead of just slugging him when he hit me in that staging post,' said Wakely. He was watching the wagon with Ed and Harriet in it disappearing into the distance. Cam was sitting on the low wall in the front of the staging-post finishing his coffee. Mr Cooper had gone to the corral at the back to fetch a horse for him. Then suddenly there came the sound of a shot. Cam slowly toppled back over the wall with blood smearing his chest.

Cam felt the excruciating pain in his chest. He knew instantly that he been shot and by whom. As a red mist appeared in front of his eyes he prayed, God, please let me stay alive to kill Wakely.

The deputy sheriff had heard the shot. He looked out through the window and saw two men mounting their horses in the distance. When they began to ride down the hill towards the staging post he rushed to get his gun from his room.

Mr Cooper's reaction was just as quick. When he heard the shot he knew that it could only mean trouble. He dropped the saddle he was holding, and rushed into the kitchen to grab his wife. 'Come on. Out the back. Quickly!' he yelled.

Cam was holding on to consciousness by a thread. He almost lost it when Wakely, instead of jumping off his horse when he reached the wall, took his horse over it in a flying leap. Sterne, who was more circumspect, jumped off his horse on the other side of the wall.

Wakely swung off his horse and aimed his revolver in a flurry of movement. Cam suddenly found his prayers answered when the mist in front of his eyes parted like the Red Sea. He could see Wakely clearly. Cam raised his pistol and fired before Wakely could aim. Cam knew that his bullet had found its target a second before he collapsed.

Sterne, who had seen the whole episode, had no wish to hang around. He knew he had $50,000 in his saddle-bag. It would be enough to keep him in luxury for a few years. He swung his horse round and was about to ride off when a voice called out, 'Sterne.'

He knew it wasn't Cam since he was either at death's gate or had already passed through it. Curiosity made him turn at the sound of his name.

The deputy sheriff was standing in the doorway holding his revolver in a hand which was bandaged and had been taken out of its sling. Normally Sterne wasn't a gambler, but the sight of the wounded lawman stirred thoughts in his mind. What were the chances of a heavily bandaged man being able to shoot straight even though he was only about fifty yards away?

'I'm taking you in,' said the deputy. 'Get down from your horse.'

Sterne decided to take the gamble. After all,

who wouldn't with $50,000 in his saddle-bag? He turned away and prepared to spur his horse. Meanwhile the gun in the deputy's hand was getting heavy to hold. He hadn't held anything since he had been shot in order to try to strengthen his muscles. His hand was already shaking with the strain when he saw Sterne turn away. The deputy put his other hand on his wrist to steady it. He fired at the split second the horse was about to move off. Sterne knew as he fell from his horse that the gamble had failed.

After glancing at Sterne's still figure, the deputy rushed to see whether Cam was still alive. To his relief he was still breathing. 'I'll fetch the doctor,' he announced.

At that moment Ed and Harriet in their wagon appeared on the scene. They had been alerted that something was wrong in the staging post by the sounds of gunfire and Harriet, thinking that somehow her boyfriend was in danger, had implored her father to turn back. As the deputy sped off to fetch the doctor Ed and Harriet set about trying to make Cam as comfortable as they could until the doctor arrived.

The stagecoach finally reached Damnation, but with a new driver and shotgun rider and with only four of the original passengers. The money was eventually returned to the stage, having

Stagecoach to Damnation

been taken from the dead bodies of Wakely and Sterne. The new bank in Damnation opened a week later than planned. Most of the inhabitants turned out for the ceremony. They saw the opening as the start of a new chapter for the town. Perhaps now the town would take its rightful place as the major town next to the Canadian border. There was already talk of the railroad reaching it the following year and before that they had been promised a telegraph system.

As a sign of the town's growing prosperity a new church was already being erected. The new preacher, Mr Beeson, stood by its side daily as he watched the progress of the builders. His wife would join him most afternoons and they would watch the builders, their hearts bursting with pride as the new edifice took shape.

The ceremony to open the bank was nothing compared to that which was held to celebrate the opening of the church. People came from all around to take part. Many people were disappointed and had to stand outside. However, the preacher left the doors open so that they could hear his service. And also so that they could hear the beautiful voice of Doris as it soared to the rafters as she thanked the Lord for delivering her husband Cam safely.

L.B.R,

XX